THE
SILENT
UNSEEN

By the Same Author

Traitor

AMANDA McCRINA

THE
SILENT
UNSEEN

FARRAR STRAUS GIROUX
NEW YORK

Farrar Straus Giroux Books for Young Readers
An imprint of Macmillan Publishing Group, LLC
120 Broadway, New York, NY 10271 • fiercereads.com

Our books may be purchased in bulk for promotional, educational, or
business use. Please contact your local bookseller or Macmillan Corporate
and Premium Sales Department at (800) 221-7945 ext. 5442 or by email at
MacmillanSpecialMarkets@macmillan.com.

Library of Congress Cataloging-in-Publication Data

Names: McCrina, Amanda, 1990– author.
Title: The silent unseen / Amanda McCrina.
Description: First edition. | New York : Farrar Straus Giroux Books for
Young Readers, [2022] | Audience: Grades 10–12. | Summary: In July
1944, as the Red Army drives the Nazis out of Poland, sixteen-year-old
Maria Kamińska must work with a captured Ukrainian nationalist to
find her brother, who is a special operations agent and leader of a Polish
Resistance squad, when he disappears while on a mission.
Identifiers: LCCN 2021025175 | ISBN 9780374313555 (hardcover)
Subjects: CYAC: Survival—Fiction. | Brothers and sisters—Fiction. |
Government, Resistance to—Fiction. | Ukrainians—Poland—Fiction. |
Poland—History—Occupation, 1939–1945—Fiction. | World War,
1939–1945—Underground movements—Poland—Fiction. | World War,
1939–1945—Atrocities—Fiction. | LCGFT: Novels. | Historical fiction.
Classification: LCC PZ7.1.M4334 Si 2022 | DDC [Fic]—dc23
LC record available at https://lccn.loc.gov/2021025175

First edition, 2022
Book design by Veronica Mang
Printed in the United States of America

1   3   5   7   9   10   8   6   4   2

For Elizabeth

On the second day after the Red Army invaded Germany, we saw eight hundred Soviet children walking eastwards on the road, the column stretching for many kilometres. Some soldiers and officers were standing by the road, peering into their faces intently and silently. They were fathers looking for their children who had been taken to Germany. One colonel had been standing there for several hours, upright, stern, with a dark, gloomy face. He went back to his car in the dusk: He hadn't found his son.

—Vasily Grossman, *A Writer at War: A Soviet Journalist with the Red Army, 1941–1945*

CONTENTS

HISTORICAL NOTE

By late July 1944, the war in Europe has been raging for nearly five years.

German forces are being pushed back on both fronts. Britain and the United States have gained a foothold in France. The Soviet Red Army, with the help of the Polish Resistance, is advancing through Poland.

As the Germans retreat west, the Soviets move to consolidate power in Poland, already anticipating a new postwar order of Soviet control over Eastern Europe. They start disarming and arresting Polish Resistance soldiers. At the same time, they begin a brutal campaign against the UPA, Ukrainian nationalist partisans attempting to carve out an independent Ukraine from Poland's disputed southeastern borderlands.

The Polish Resistance and the UPA have fought each other bitterly and bloodily through the years of German occupation. Historic grievances and injustices have become excuses for atrocities. Civilians have suffered the brunt of it. Tens of thousands have died—Polish civilians in massacres by the UPA, Ukrainian civilians in targeted reprisals by the Resistance. Now both sides, Polish and Ukrainian, face the prospect of another long occupation, another long war against another oppressive regime.

Both sides look to the western Allies for help against the Soviets once Germany is finally defeated. But western help is months away—if it comes at all.

Neither can afford to wait that long.

And neither can hope to win this war alone.

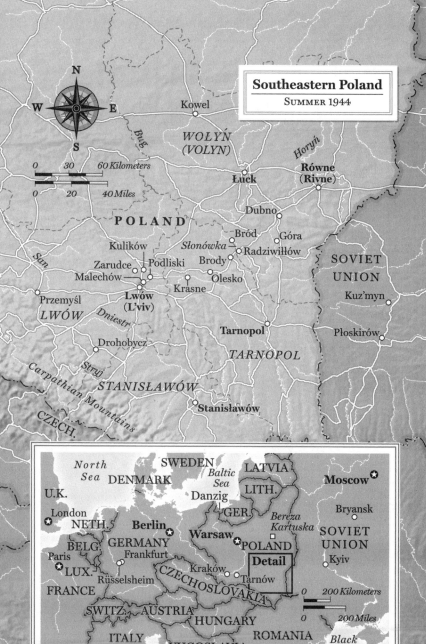

N
W E
S

0   30   60 Kilometers
0   20   40 Miles

Kowel

WOŁYŃ
(VOLYN)

Bug

Horyń

Łuck

Równe
(Rivne)

POLAND

Dubno

Bród   Góra
Słonówka   Radziwiłłów
Kulików   Brody
Zarudce   Podliski
Malechów   Olesko
Lwów   Krasne
(L'viv)

San

SOVIET
UNION

Kuz'myn

Płoskirów

Przemyśl

LWÓW

Dniestr

Tarnopol

Drohobycz

TARNOPOL

Stryj

Carpathian Mountains

STANISŁAWÓW

CZECH.

Stanisławów

North
Sea   SWEDEN   LATVIA
DENMARK   Baltic
Sea   LITH.   Moscow

U.K.   Danzig   GER.
London   NETH.   Berlin   Bereza
Kartuska   SOVIET
UNION
BELG.   GERMANY   Warsaw
Paris   Frankfurt   POLAND   Kyiv
LUX.   Rüsselsheim   Detail   Bryansk
FRANCE   CZECHOSLOVAKIA   Kraków
SWITZ.   AUSTRIA   Tarnów
ITALY   HUNGARY   ROMANIA   0   200 Kilometers
YUGOSLAVIA   Black
Sea   0   200 Miles

Map by Gene Thorp

THE
SILENT
UNSEEN

1
MARIA

LWÓW, POLAND
FRIDAY, JULY 28, 1944

SOMEBODY HAD SHOT A POLITICAL OFFICER.

At least—I thought. My Russian wasn't anything at all to be proud of. But I had been handcuffed to this chair in this office listening to the junior officer out at the front desk shout into a telephone for over an hour, and I was pretty sure that was what he was saying between expletives: Somebody murdered a *zampolit* last night—yes, murder—shot twice from behind at close range.

The culprit seemed to be one of their own men, which meant it wasn't me. I doubted I would be *here*, sitting relatively comfortably in this office, if they thought it was me.

My pistol, the Walther they took off me when they arrested me this morning, sat on the desk in front of me, pointing at me accusingly. It was half the reason I was here—carrying a weapon without authorization—and I guessed it was in here as evidence. It was the *only* thing I was carrying, which was the other half of the reason. I didn't have any papers. I had a perfectly valid excuse, but so far nobody had been interested in listening to it. Everybody had just assumed I was Polish Resistance—a courier, perhaps, and apparently stupid enough to blunder right into a Soviet patrol.

The problem was I didn't know how to prove I *wasn't*. I knew enough about Soviet justice to know you were guilty until proven innocent. Sometimes even then.

The desk belonged to Comrade Colonel F. Volkov, 64th Rifle Division, NKVD. There was a nameplate. There were also two photographs in frames—I didn't know of what; they weren't facing me—and a fountain pen in a holder, all precisely arranged. The drab green papered walls were empty, though you could see the odd dark spot here and there where previous occupants had hung things. They were still clearing out this place from the German occupation. Lwów had been in Soviet hands for all of twenty-four hours. The dust hadn't even settled.

Somebody shut the office door behind me, muffling the sound of the ongoing telephone call.

Comrade Colonel F. Volkov came around the desk, unbuttoning his coat. He folded the coat neatly over the back of his chair, laid his briefcase on the desk, and set his smart blue cap beside it just so. Then he sat down facing me. He didn't look at me yet. He opened his briefcase and took out a piece of paper—my arrest report, I presumed—and spent a minute reading it in silence.

I knew how these things worked. I could guarantee you he had already read it. This part was just for show. But I wasn't complaining. It gave me a chance to size him up. I would put him at thirty-five or forty, prematurely gray, handsome in a stiff, austere sort of way—absolutely unremarkable to all appearances, but I knew better. You didn't get to be comrade colonel of the NKVD by being unremarkable.

"Maria Kamińska," he read aloud.

"*Da.*"

"You may speak in Polish," he said disinterestedly, not looking up. "Tell me if I need to make any corrections. Polish national, sixteen years old, resident of Bród, arrested for unauthorized possession of a weapon." He eyed the pistol just briefly. It was a German pistol, the Walther, which I assumed was doubly suspicious. "No identification."

"Yes—I mean, no corrections."

"Where is Bród?"

I didn't blame him for having to ask. There were about thirty-seven little villages called Bród in Poland. *Bród* just meant "river ford." It was the sort of name I *would* make up if I were a spy or something.

"On the Słonówka River in Wołyń Province," I told him. "Ten kilometers from Radziwiłłów." Four days' walk east of here. I didn't have a map, but I had divided the distance up by days on the big map in the train station back in Tarnów.

I couldn't tell whether the names meant anything to him. His face was expressionless. "Why are you in Lwów?"

I wasn't, technically. They had arrested me on the road west of the city. But I didn't think *Because your men brought me here* was the answer he was looking for.

"I'm just trying to go home," I said.

"Home from where?"

"Rüsselsheim—in Germany. The Opel automobile plant there. I was—"

"*Ostarbeiter*. Taken for slave labor." He looked up for the first time. There was something almost hungry in the way his eyes searched over my face. "You escaped?"

"During the bombing. There was an air raid—the Americans. The overseers left our barracks unguarded while they were in the bomb shelters. I started running."

"You've come from Rüsselsheim on foot?" He sounded more surprised than suspicious.

"Just from Tarnów. That's where the rail lines stopped. I hopped trains from Frankfurt."

He took out his fountain pen and made a note in Russian in the margin of the paper. "How long since you were taken?"

"Two and a half years."

The pen paused.

"That winter—after the invasion." I was careful not to say the

German invasion, which would draw awkward attention to the fact that there had also been a Soviet one. I didn't want to do anything to antagonize this man. "February twenty-third, 1942." I had held on to that date. I had held on to the memory of that morning—the last time I saw my parents' faces. I had been so afraid I would forget their faces.

Comrade Colonel F. Volkov put his pen down.

"You may find," he said carefully, "very much has changed in two and a half years."

Dear God, did he think I hadn't thought about that?

"I know," I said.

"I wouldn't go any farther east," he said.

There was a warning in his voice. It made my heart clench like a fist. "But—"

"I'll write you a pass." He opened a desk drawer. "Turn around. Go to Przemyśl. Register with the Red Cross there. It's possible they may be able to put you in touch with any of your family who might—"

He cut himself short, but I knew what he was going to say.

Who might still be alive.

It had been two and a half years. I wasn't stupid. I had heard the stories. I knew what the Germans had done to my people, to his people. There were Russian *Ostarbeiter* with me in the Opel plant.

"But I've come all this way." Helplessly, I watched him take out another piece of paper and pick up his pen. It was a struggle to keep my voice steady. Not like this—not when I was so close.

He wasn't listening. He wasn't looking at me anymore. His head was bent as he wrote. The conversation was apparently over as far as he was concerned.

"Please." Maybe I *was* stupid. He was letting me go—didn't even ask any questions about the gun—and I was arguing with him. Not even arguing. Grasping for any and every little excuse like a little kid who couldn't take no for an answer. "All I need is a few more days."

He opened another drawer and took out an ink pad and a rubber stamp. He inked a bloodred hammer-and-sickle seal on the corner of the paper. "Whatever you might find in Bród—I can guarantee it's not what you want to find."

I tried to shrug indifferently. It was awkward with my arms spread, wrists cuffed to the chair arms. "It's still home."

He didn't look up. "Not anymore. Not the home you knew."

"I promised. I told them I would come back." My throat was tight—anger and desperation and hopelessness all at once. I swallowed fiercely. I was *not* going to cry. "Please. Just four more days."

He sighed just audibly. He returned the stamp to the drawer. He slid the paper across the desk toward me under his fingertips.

"You may use it as you wish," he said, "but my recommendation is that you go to Przemyśl."

"Thank you," I breathed.

He ignored that. "Since you're not going to take my recommendation, consider this a warning." His voice was cold. "This is still contested territory. A pass from me is a death sentence in the wrong hands. UPA or Resistance thugs won't care that you're a civilian."

"I know." At least—I knew what he meant by Resistance. There had been a Polish Resistance squad in the wood outside Bród. A few of them were Polish army soldiers who had avoided internment or deportation under the Soviets during the first invasion, the 1939 invasion. Most of them were boys from Bród who had slipped one by one into the wood in the weeks and months that followed.

I had no idea what he meant by UPA. Another partisan group? The only other partisans I knew of were the Soviet ones—escaped POWs, stragglers left behind when the Germans invaded in 1941. They couldn't be who he meant—not if he was calling them thugs.

He pushed his chair back and came around the desk, taking a key from his pocket. He unlocked my handcuffs and dumped them on the desk. He didn't move right away, so I was still trapped in the chair, suddenly aware of how close he was—suddenly aware that it was entirely possible he was expecting a little favor in return.

Panic roiled my stomach. I fought it down, gripping the chair arms. *Breathe. Think.* My pistol was still there on the desk. I doubted it was loaded, but you could bet I would make it do some damage.

He didn't touch me. He wasn't even looking at me. He reached across the desk for one of the framed photographs. I let go of the chair arms slowly, cautiously. My heart was racing.

He held the photograph in his hands for a second. His shoulders were stiff.

"If you could tell me——" he started.

He didn't finish. He turned the photograph around to show me. It was just a snapshot, a slightly blurry personal snapshot—not something you would expect to see framed, under glass. There was a boy of ten or twelve trying to make the obviously struggling white kitten on his lap pose for the camera. The boy wasn't really looking at the camera. He was looking at the kitten, the corner of his mouth quirked up in a lopsided smile. I imagined the person holding the camera was laughing; that was why it was blurry.

Comrade Colonel F. Volkov watched my face expectantly, waiting for a reaction.

"Your son?" I managed politely.

Obviously not what he was hoping for. His face was blank, but his shoulders dropped just a little.

"Nikolai," he said. He set the photograph on the desk. "He's older now—he would be older now." He corrected himself absently. "He would be fifteen." He looked away. "He was taken last summer. I thought it might be possible that you might have—— that you might know——"

I picked up the photograph and looked at it again. I knew for a fact I hadn't seen this boy before—the boys in the plant had all been Poles or Ukrainians, at least the ones who worked in my section—but I didn't want him to think I was just brushing him off.

"Nikolai Fyodorovich," he told me. His gaze came back to me, sharp and hopeful. "From Bryansk."

Bryansk was in western Russia. I remembered the name. I remembered the snippets of news bulletins we caught on our contraband wireless that autumn after the German invasion. The Germans had hoped to take Moscow before winter set in. The offensive had stalled at Bryansk—just for two weeks, but two weeks was enough. The Germans had taken Bryansk. They hadn't ever taken Moscow.

I held the photograph up as if I were trying to see it in better light. I wanted to lie to him. I wanted to say, *Yes, I remember, I saw him.* I knew his grief, his pain. I knew it because I had felt it the day we found out my brother, Tomek, was dead. I knew it because I had seen it in my parents' faces the morning the soldiers came for me.

I knew why he was letting me go home to Bród.

I shook my head and put the photograph back on the desk.

"I'm sorry." It came out in a whisper. My throat was tight again. "There were other factories—other camps—"

He nodded once.

"Yes," he said, with practiced detachment. "It would have been statistically unlikely."

He placed the photograph very carefully back in its original position, at an exact ninety-degree angle against the other photograph. Then he picked up my pistol and the stamped paper and handed them to me one after the other.

"My adjutant will show you out," he said.

2
KOSTYA

L'VIV, POLAND

THURSDAY, JULY 27, 1944

TWELVE HOURS SINCE THE REDS ENTERED L'VIV.
Kostya had been waiting at this bar for six.

Nobody had really noticed him yet. Just another uniform
nursing a bottle. If somebody had been paying attention, somebody would have known he'd been nursing the same bottle of
vodka all afternoon, and somebody might have started to get suspicious. But nobody was paying attention. Red soldiers drifted
in, out, on to the next bar. The barman, a spectacled old relic
from another time in apron and white jacket, wasn't asking for
money from anybody—in heartfelt Soviet camaraderie or maybe
just because he didn't want to get shot. He seemed happy to
leave Kostya alone.

The problem was the place was starting to fill up.

It was past six o'clock, and Red infantry had been pouring into the city all day. Bits and pieces of the 60th Army, most of them, but Kostya had seen some NKVD too—secret police. The NKVD made him nervous. Sooner or later, somebody was going to slide in beside him at the bar and try to strike up a conversation, which would be a disaster. His Russian was pretty good—still slightly accented but nothing anybody would think twice about. But he'd been counting on having a little more time to work on particulars before actually having to *use* them. He felt unprepared—too visible, too vulnerable.

When you were unprepared, you made mistakes. And when you made mistakes, you were dead.

The fake Soviet papers in his stolen uniform jacket's breast pocket said he was Valerik Fialko, Second Battalion, 100th Rifle Division. If somebody from the Second—somebody *else* from the Second, better get that straight right now—came in here and started asking questions, he'd give himself maybe five minutes before he was kissing a wall with a gun against the base of his skull.

What kind of idiot picks this for a meeting place anyway?

The same kind of idiot who volunteered to be a UPA mole in a Red Army front, Kostya guessed.

He had no idea what his contact looked like. Didn't know his name either. Whoever he was, he'd been the one to initiate proceedings, and he'd at least been smart enough not to do it directly. The message had come in code through Commander Shukhevych's headquarters over in Volyn. No time, just *Afternoon*

27th. Place, password, countersign, brief instructions: *Take off your cap, fold it in your belt.*

That was it.

He would give it ten more minutes—half past. Then he was out of here. They would try again another day, and this time *he* was going to pick the place.

He poured one more glass and took a last opportunity to survey the room while he tipped it back. Another pack of soldiers was straggling in from the street. There weren't enough open tables. Four or five of them broke away to come stand at the bar. Kostya pretended to be lost in his glass. *Damn it.* The more and more groups that came in, the more and more obvious it was going to be that he was alone. Being alone invited questions.

"Pour me one, Comrade?"

Like that.

He set his glass down a little too forcefully. She didn't seem to notice. She smiled at him. There were sergeant's straps on the shoulders of her uniform tunic. The Mosin rifle across her back had been retrofitted for sniping. Blond hair pulled into a neat, tight bun, cool eyes somewhere between green and brown and gray. Older than he was but not by much. He guessed she was twenty.

She crooked an elbow on the counter—close enough to brush his arm, far enough away to pretend it was an accident.

"You look like you could use a friend," she said.

Kostya reached across the counter for another glass. *Wonderful.*

She'd said comrade, but she wore sergeant's straps. Rank meant something even to the Reds. He was Valerik Fialko, Second Battalion nonentity. He couldn't ignore her, and he couldn't just brush her off—not without risking a scene. People would start noticing. People would remember.

What kind of IDIOT picks this for a meeting place?

He filled the glass and slid it to her, giving her a teeth-bared grin.

"Who needs friends? I've got vodka."

She leaned in conspiratorially. Her voice was an exaggerated whisper. "Why settle for one when you could have both?"

"Because now I've got to share my vodka, Comrade Sergeant," he said.

She laughed. "True." She lifted her glass, brushing his arm again. Vodka sloshed over the countertop.

Kostya stiffened. She wasn't as drunk as she was acting, which meant—

"*Slava Ukrayini,*" she murmured, tossing the vodka back with a practiced flick of her wrist.

Glory to Ukraine.

For a second, he was too startled to do anything but stare. Then he remembered.

"*Heroyam s-slava,*" he stammered. Glory to her heroes.

Password, countersign.

"Good job." She set her glass down delicately on the countertop.

"Relax, Comrade. Put your arm around me. Try to look like you're having fun."

Obediently, he draped an arm across her shoulders, pulling her close. She nestled her face into his neck. Her fingers slid through his hair, pulling his head down so she could murmur into his ear.

"What's your name?"

Her lips tickled his earlobe. He closed his eyes, willing himself not to shiver. *Not* the way he'd been expecting this to go. "Valerik. You?"

"Nataliya." She slid an arm around his neck, pressing her cheek to his. "Let's get a few things straight, all right, Valerik? First, this is strictly professional, so don't get any ideas. I promise I've got no problem shooting you. Got it?"

"Yes."

"Second, I've set up a cache for you under the bench across the square—third from the end of the row, by the lamppost. Most of our communication will go through there. The less we have to meet, the better. I'll find you if I need you."

"Could have said all that in your message." Kostya rested his free hand on the counter. His pistol was inside his tunic. He couldn't get to it the way she was pressed against him, which meant she knew it was there too. He was acutely aware of her arm around his neck. "So tell me why I'm really here."

She turned her head under his chin and leaned her ear on his chest as though she were listening for his heartbeat. "Nice work. You're not as stupid as you look."

Except he was. He should have known Kyrylo would sell him out. He should have known this was a setup.

Damn it, he should have known that was why Marko had sent *him*.

He had walked right into it. He had stood here waiting for it.

She must have felt him tense. She let out a breath of a laugh. "Don't worry. It's a pretty public place for a murder."

"What do you want?"

"Not to kill you, just so we're clear—though now I'm wondering why that would be your first assumption. Guilty conscience?"

Kostya didn't say anything.

"Relax, Valerik. It was a joke." She glanced up. "First time out?"

"Yes," he lied.

"It gets easier," she said.

Her voice was low—almost gentle. It threw him. He looked away. His chest was stupidly tight.

"You haven't answered my question," he said.

Her fingers played absently with the buttons at the throat of his tunic. "You're here because I've got a message for Marko that I didn't want to send through the regular channels."

"Why not?"

"If I told you, I'd have to kill you." She stood up on her toes, looped both arms around his neck, and kissed him very softly on the cheek. "Thanks for sharing your vodka, Comrade. Watch the cache."

"That's the message?"

She lifted her arms away. "And you were doing so well." She patted his chest. "Pocket. It's coded, but I'd still recommend trying not to get caught with it."

* * *

"I was beginning to think you'd gone to Marko and ratted me out," Kyrylo said. "Either that or you were dead—and of the two of those, I can guarantee you'd rather be dead."

Kyrylo—code name Lys, the Fox—was Kostya's cousin. He sat at the dining room table, fiddling with the same dead radio he'd been fiddling with for two weeks, adrift in a sea of pliers and screwdrivers and spare wires under a thick fog of cigarette smoke. He liked to think he knew things about electronics, and about fixing electronics, which was stupid—almost as stupid as his code name. Kostya was pretty sure he'd never touched a tool in his life before he joined the UPA. He'd been studying to be a lawyer, eventually to be a politician, eventually to be a revolutionary.

Kyrylo also liked to say things like *You ratted me out* and *You'd rather be dead*, like some gangster in a pulp magazine, which was even stupider. You could hear money and privilege and a university education in his voice. He just sounded like an idiot, trying to talk street tough.

He wasn't an idiot; that was the thing.

Lots of people got that wrong about Kyrylo. Lots of people thought that was all he was—talk, empty threats. Lots of people probably thought they knew the type.

Lots of those people were dead.

"I'm not a rat," Kostya said coldly.

"Technically you are, but it was a joke. Lighten up, kid. How'd it go?"

Kostya dragged another chair up to the table. He took the sealed paper from his breast pocket and shoved it at Kyrylo without a word. *Kid* grated too. At seventeen, he wasn't all that much younger than his cousin—five years. The way Kyrylo liked to talk, you'd think it was twenty.

Kyrylo reached for the paper. "Who's the contact?"

"Her name's Nataliya. She's undercover as a junior sergeant with the Hundredth Rifles."

"And the cache?"

"Podwale Street," Kostya recited, "third bench from the end of the row, under the lamppost."

"You'd better not be lying to me." Kyrylo slit the seal neatly with a thumbnail, unfolded the paper, and smoothed it out over the tabletop. "Did you read it?"

"It's coded."

Kyrylo rolled his eyes. He sent the paper back to Kostya under his fingertips. "Here. You can do it faster than I can."

That was a lie, and they both knew it. Kostya resisted the urge to crush the paper in his fist and throw it at Kyrylo's head.

"I don't think I'm supposed to know what it says," he said tightly.

Kyrylo snorted. "So? Neither am I."

"You're an officer. Marko's probably going to tell you what it says anyway. I'm just——"

"In as deep as I am," Kyrylo finished. "Come on, Kostya. Don't you want to know what you risked your life for?"

"What *you* risked my life for," Kostya snapped.

Kyrylo's eyes narrowed. "I don't decide the missions."

"You're the one who gave me to Marko in the first place. You're the one——"

"I didn't give you to Marko. He picked you because you're reliable, trustworthy, wise as a serpent, innocent as a dove——"

"Shut up."

"Need to work on the sense of humor, though." Kyrylo turned the radio over in his hands, trying to balance it on his knee while he reattached the back panel. "Read me the message, Kostek, or you don't get paid this month."

Kostya snatched the paper back. "Don't call me Kostek."

"Then read me the message, Kostyantyn Vitaliyovych Lasko."

It would be a miracle if he didn't kill Kyrylo himself before this war was over. His cousin was a true believer, a convinced nationalist. He'd joined the UPA, the Ukrainian Insurgent Army, so he could help build a new, independent Ukraine, a pure-blooded Ukraine, free of Poles and Soviets alike. Kostya had joined because it was that or a bullet—Marko and Kyrylo had made the choice very clear—and even so, Mama would break his head if she knew. He hadn't dared go back home to Bród these past two and a half years, even on leave. He just sent the money every month and prayed Mama would pretend ignorance about where it came from. His sister Lesya had probably made up some story to try to cover for him: He'd made it away to Turkey and was working on a fishing boat; he'd followed the Vistula up to Danzig and gotten across to Sweden.

Mama had probably seen right through it. She always did.

Kostya flipped to a fresh page in his notebook. This month, the messages had started being keyed to Lenin's *The State and Revolution*—harmless enough to have lying around if the Reds came looking. They'd been keyed to German texts before this: anti-Jewish and anti-communist propaganda mostly, or Ukrainian translations of important Nazi speeches. Sick stuff. The call to worldwide violent revolution seemed almost tame by comparison.

"Did you eat?" Kyrylo asked, still busily turning screws on the panel.

Kostya ignored him. He hadn't eaten since breakfast, which

had been one piece of black bread and one piece of cold *salo*, fatback. But pretending-to-care Kyrylo was just as bad as trying-to-sound-like-a-tough-guy Kyrylo.

"Aw, somebody's sore," Kyrylo said.

"Shut up."

"Hey." Kyrylo's voice sharpened. "Watch the attitude."

"I'm not your kid."

"No. But I outrank you, and I can have you shot—and I will if you ever talk to me like that in front of my men."

"Fascist prick." Kostya scraped his chair back, shoving the notebook away. "Decode your own damn message."

"Hey, Kostya. Kostya." Kyrylo dumped the radio on the table and got up. Screws and washers and loose wires scattered in his wake. He stepped into Kostya's path, throwing an arm across the doorway before Kostya could duck past him. "All right. Enough. Tell me what's going on."

"Let me go."

"Did something happen at the bar?"

Kostya flung Kyrylo's arm away. "I got the message, didn't I?"

"That wasn't the question, genius." Kyrylo clapped both hands on Kostya's shoulders and pushed him back against the wall, hard. "Tell me what happened."

Kostya didn't even *know* what had happened; that was the problem. Something about the way he'd thought—just for a second—he'd been sent to that bar for his own execution. Something about the way Nataliya had said, *It gets easier.*

It never got any easier. You just got more careful.

He was tired of having to be careful.

"I want out," he said.

He didn't even know that was what was going to come out until it did.

Kyrylo didn't say anything.

"I'm sick of it." Kostya's throat was tight. Damn it, he was *not* going to cry in front of Kyrylo. "I'm sick of having to watch my back. I'm sick of waiting for that bullet. I want out."

"It's not that easy," Kyrylo said quietly.

"'I outrank you. I can have you shot.' Sounded pretty easy to me."

For a second, Kyrylo just scowled at him. Then he said, "Give me your pistol."

"Go to hell."

Kyrylo didn't even blink. He yanked open Kostya's tunic with one quick hand, tore the pistol from the shoulder holster, and tossed it across the room.

Over his shoulder, he said, "Dima."

His second-in-command loomed in the kitchen doorway. He was smirking. He'd probably been listening to every word. "Sir?"

"Busy?"

"No, sir."

"Then you can take baby to his room." Kyrylo tousled Kostya's hair, then shoved him toward the doorway. "Make sure he gets his nap and his bottle and doesn't do anything stupid. I know it'll be hard for him."

Kostya lunged. Dima snaked a quick, strong arm around him, jerking him back so sharply that his breath whooshed out. Tiny white stars danced across the room.

"Coward," Kostya spit. It came out in a squeak. Dima's arm was like a steel bar across his stomach. "Go ahead—have me shot. Can't even do it yourself, can you?"

"Feel free to shut him up." Kyrylo was already back in his chair, the radio on his lap.

"Do you mean shut him up?" Dima clamped a hand over Kostya's mouth. "Or *shut him up*?" He made a pistol with his free hand and touched Kostya's temple with his fingertips.

"Start with the first one. I'd hate to have to write *that* letter to Aunt Klara."

"I'll talk," Kostya snarled around Dima's fingers. "I'll tell Marko. I'll tell him you've been reading the messages. I'll tell him—"

"Get him out of here before I change my mind," Kyrylo said.

* * *

His room was four blank brick walls and a concrete floor and a single bare electric bulb hung on a wire from the ceiling. He had his old quilt for a bedroll and a line to hang his change of clothes, and he had his name saint, the Roman emperor Constantine, on an icon stuck in a chink in the wall where a bit of grout had come loose. He'd had a photograph of the family—all of them, Papa, Mama, Lesya, Lyudya, and him, the baby—but Kyrylo had taken that away from him as soon as he'd seen it and thrown it into the kitchen stove.

"What are you—stupid?" he'd snapped. "What if the Poles or the Germans found that?"

Papa was already dead by then, and Lyudya was gone, taken by the Germans. It had been the only copy of the photograph.

That was the first time he'd ever wanted to kill Kyrylo.

The door was locked. He'd tried it. He was pretty sure this used to be a pantry—you could see holes in the brick where the shelves had been drilled in—and it locked from the outside. It doubled as a cell sometimes when Kyrylo was holding a prisoner for questioning. When that happened, Kostya slept on the floor by the kitchen stove, trying not to listen while Kyrylo did the interrogation. Kyrylo always handled the interrogations himself because he spoke all four languages fluently— Polish, German, Russian, Ukrainian. Nobody else in the squad knew German, and most of them wouldn't speak Polish or Russian on principle.

He could hear Dima whistling out in the kitchen, clattering pans and chopping something on a board. The smell of frying sausages and onions drifted in through the cracks around the door. It was Dima and Yuliya's flat technically—or it was old Mrs. Baranets's technically, but Mrs. Baranets let her grandson Dima and his wife use it, and Dima and Yuliya let Kyrylo use it as his safe house. They'd all met at university, Dima and Yuliya and Kyrylo. Kostya was the stupid one. *Selyuk*, Dima called him. Peasant. He didn't mean anything by it, Kyrylo said. But they all laughed when he said it, as if it were some joke they all knew and Kostya didn't.

The lock rattled.

Kostya had just enough time to flop down on his quilt, face to the wall, eyes squeezed shut, before the door swung open. He'd been expecting Dima, bringing dinner, but he could hear Dima still whistling out in the kitchen when the door creaked shut again.

"Kostya," Kyrylo said.

Kostya lay very still.

"Come on, idiot, I know you're not asleep. The light's on."

The trick was the way you breathed—long and slow in, long and slow out . . .

Kyrylo's boot jabbed him roughly in the ribs. "All right. Up. You've got a date, remember?"

Long and slow in, long and slow out . . .

Kyrylo reached down without another word, hauled Kostya up by his collar, slammed him into the wall, and pinned him there, one hand clamped on Kostya's throat.

He slid Nataliya's paper, carefully resealed, into the front of Kostya's tunic.

"Good as new," he said, giving the tunic a little tug to straighten it.

"Get your hands off me."

"One more little thing, Kostek, before you go—about what you said back there." Kyrylo's fingers tightened on Kostya's throat. "You say these things sometimes, and I don't know if you're really serious or if you're just trying to push my buttons. So—a reminder. Just to make sure we've both got it straight."

He bent close. His voice was low—dangerously low and calm.

"If you ever breathe a word to Marko—if you ever so much as *think* about breathing a word to Marko—I will kill Aunt Klara and Lesya. I will make you watch while I do it. Then I will kill you. Do you understand me?"

This—this was what everybody got wrong about Kyrylo. You didn't think he *could*. He was too cultured, too educated, too well-dressed, too proper, too polite, too charming, to be the sort of guy who would put a bullet in your head once he'd extracted your gasped and whimpering confession.

"Yes, sir," Kostya said.

Kyrylo's fingers tightened a little more. "Look at me."

Kostya looked. "Yes, sir," he said.

"All of it, Kostek."

"Yes, sir, I understand you," Kostya said obediently.

"Good." Kyrylo shoved him away. "Clean yourself up before you go. I swear you always look like you've just crawled back from a damn bar fight."

3
KOSTYA

"YOU'RE LATE, VALERIK," MARKO SAID.

He was waiting at the far end of the crypt—sitting at the map table with a squad leader Kostya didn't recognize, watching while Kostya hurried down the steps.

He was furious. His flinty blue eyes cut Kostya up and down like knives.

"You're late," he repeated. "Why?"

The crypt was empty except for the three of them. Kostya's footsteps echoed loudly in the silence—across the flagged floor, up the shadowed walls, away across the vaulted ceiling. His planned excuse—one of the usual, that he'd had to backtrack to avoid a patrol—died to ashes on his tongue. He wasn't that late. The clock over at City Hall hadn't even tolled a quarter past ten yet, so at worst he was less than fifteen minutes late—which meant Marko had dismissed everybody else deliberately.

Which meant this was all deliberate—theatrical and deliberate, like a show trial.

Marko's red-stubbled face was wreathed in cigarette smoke and lit up ghoulishly by the dim, flickering light of the tallow candles in the niches. There wasn't any electricity in the church, not since the Reds' initial artillery barrage last week. There probably wouldn't be electricity any time soon. That wasn't, Kostya assumed, very high on the Reds' priority list, even if they let Father Kliment keep the church open—and if they did let him keep it open, Kyrylo said, it meant they had it under surveillance. Marko was an idiot to keep using it as his headquarters in any case. But it made a very good headquarters because the crypt was as secure as a bomb shelter and you could see pretty much all of L'viv from the bell tower.

He was intimidating on a good day, Marko—two full meters of solid muscle. On a bad day, he was a live grenade. Kostya hated him. Before Commander Shukhevych had made him leader of L'viv Group, he—like Commander Shukhevych—had been one of the Nachtigallen, Ukrainian volunteers in the German army. As far as Kostya was concerned, that made him equally guilty for what they'd done to Lyudya.

Today was apparently a bad day, because of course it was. Kostya could practically feel the air bristling.

"I asked you a question," Marko said.

Kostya saluted, slipped Nataliya's message from inside his tunic, and stepped up hastily to lay it on the table. He was still catching his breath. The words came out in a stammer. "I-I'm sorry, sir. Took longer at the b-bar than I—"

"Stop stammering."

"Yes, sir. I'm sorry, sir."

Kostya *hated* him.

Marko stuck his cigarette in his mouth and reached for the message. This was the point at which Kostya would usually be dismissed. He was a glorified errand boy; his part was over as soon as the message, whatever it was, was safely in Marko's hands. But Marko didn't make any move to dismiss him. He pulled on his cigarette, flipped open the message with one thick finger, and started reading. He didn't even seem to notice Kostya still standing there. The squad leader beside him was playing with a flip lighter—flicking the wheel absently with a thumbnail over and over, not looking up.

Deliberate, all of it—and stupid. The message was coded. There was no way Marko was actually reading it.

Kostya studied his boots, trying to look appropriately humble. "Sir, if there's anything else—"

Marko tossed the message away and stubbed his cigarette out all at once.

"Come here for a second," he said.

Kostya froze. "Sir?"

"Come here." Marko scraped his chair back and got up,

beckoning with two fingers. He took Kostya's elbow and pulled him over. He jerked his chin. "Have you met Solovey?"

Kostya swallowed. He'd heard of him, of course—the squad leader who'd once lined up twelve Polish prisoners and shot them in the head one by one. That was the standard version anyway. The numbers changed. Sometimes it was a whole platoon, and he'd had to stop to reload four times. "No, sir."

"Valerik," Marko informed Solovey, clapping a meaty hand on Kostya's shoulder.

Solovey glanced up from his lighter. His cold gray eyes met Kostya's just for a second. "Valerik. The stammerer. Got it."

Kostya's face burned. *Bastard.*

"Tell me something, Valerik." Marko pulled him close. "Where was the bar?"

"Sir?"

"The bar where you met our informant. Where was it?"

Kostya licked his dry lips. "Across the square, sir."

"How far from here, roughly? A hundred meters? A hundred and fifty?"

Solovey was lighting a cigarette. Kostya focused intently on the winking red tip. "I don't know, sir."

"Tell me you're not that stupid. Guess."

"A hundred and fifty meters, sir."

Marko's fingers dug into his shoulder, hard. "So tell me why Solovey saw you in Łyczakowski half an hour ago."

Kostya opened his mouth.

Nothing came out.

He knew. *He knew*.

Marko's fist smashed into Kostya's face. "Answer me, you piece of shit."

"Had to b-backtrack—"

Another blow. The room spun. The lit tip of Solovey's cigarette was going around and around and around in little flaming circles.

"You stammered," Marko said.

Kostya clenched his teeth. Hot blood dribbled over his lips. "There was a Red patrol. They were asking for papers. Didn't want to risk it with the message on me. I had to go all the way around."

"You went to Lys, didn't you? You took the message to Lys."

"There was a patrol," Kostya repeated, teeth gritted. "I had to go around."

Another blow. "You went to Lys."

"I had to go around."

Another blow. He was on his knees.

Marko took out his pistol, snapped the action, and pressed the cold mouth to the back of Kostya's skull.

"Ten seconds. Then I'll kill you. Then I'll kill your traitor cousin. Or you can tell me the truth."

It's just a test. He's guessing. He doesn't know.

"Nine," Marko said.

If he knew, he'd have killed you already.

"Eight."

The only way he knows is if you tell him—if you break.

"Seven."

Just like the training.

"Six."

Just like the training.

"Five."

It's a test.

"Four."

It's a test.

"Three."

It's a test.

"Two."

But if it isn't.

"One," Marko said.

Silence. The pistol sat cold and hard against the back of Kostya's skull. He waited.

"I can protect them, Valerik," Marko said.

He didn't dare move. He didn't dare breathe.

"Your mother," Marko said, "your sister. I can protect them."

It was a trick. It had to be a trick.

Didn't it?

Marko lifted the pistol away from Kostya's head.

"Just give me the truth, Valerik. All you have to do is give me the truth."

Maybe he'd just passed the test.

He licked blood from his lips and swallowed.

"And you'll protect them," he said.

"I'll protect them," Marko said.

Kostya squeezed his eyes shut.

"Didn't have a choice." The words felt funny coming out—slurred and shapeless, all mashed together. His tongue was thick. His mouth was full of blood and loose teeth. "He said he would kill them. Said he would kill them unless I gave him the messages and code keys. I didn't have a choice."

Marko's voice was quiet. "How long?"

"The whole time. The whole time I've been on the circuit."

"Two years."

"Yes, sir."

Marko's hand settled on his shoulder, his thumb brushing gently across the back of Kostya's neck.

"Two years you could have come to me," he said.

Kostya opened his eyes. *Wait.*

"Radio Bród," Marko said to Solovey over Kostya's head. "Tell them to make an example. I don't want any more of these rat problems."

"And Lys?" Solovey asked. He was leaning against the table, pulling lazily on his cigarette. His eyes rested levelly on Kostya's.

"Bring him. Now."

"Here?"

WAIT.

Kostya tried to lunge up. Marko shoved him back down.

The pistol jabbed sharply against his skull, forcing his head down.

"You said all I had to do was give you the truth." It came out in a whisper. His throat was tight with panic. An uncontrollable shiver had started somewhere deep inside him. "You said—"

"You could have come to me, Valerik. You didn't. That makes you complicit."

"He said he would kill them. He said if I ever breathed a word—"

"Then they would have died as patriots." Marko looked up at Solovey. "I said bring Lys."

Solovey took out his cigarette unhurriedly and blew a soft, smoky breath. He flicked his fingers at the pistol. "I wouldn't do that here."

"Sound's not going to carry."

"What are you going to do with the bodies?"

Marko didn't say anything.

Solovey stubbed out his cigarette against the butt of his holstered pistol.

"I'll take care of it," he said. "Outside the city. Both of them."

4
KOSTYA

THEY HAD BEEN DRIVING FOR A LONG TIME—
longer than Kostya had expected.

Or maybe it just seemed that way given the circumstances. He didn't know. He was curled up on the back seat, hands cuffed tightly behind his back, sweating under an NKVD officer's heavy woolen coat. There was a twisted bundle of handkerchiefs stuffed halfway down his throat. They didn't seem to care as much about him suffocating as about making sure he did it out of sight and quietly.

He'd made one panicked, desperate attempt to get away right outside the church, jerking his head back into Solovey's face and stomping Solovey's foot under the heel of his boot.

Andriy, Solovey's second-in-command, had opened the car door smoothly right in front of him just as he started running. He'd hit the door, then the pavement—hard. He'd still been dizzy and wheezing when they shoved the gag in his mouth, threw the coat over him, and tossed him into the back seat like a sack of potatoes.

He could hear them talking quietly to each other every so often. They'd left the paved road a while back. The car bounced and jolted over rutted gravel. They were somewhere north of the city—he'd felt it when they went over the railway crossing what seemed like hours ago—but north of the city could be a lot of places, and he didn't know any of them very well. He wasn't from here the way Kyrylo and the rest of them were. He had run messages to some of the UPA forest squads occasionally when there wasn't anybody else, but he'd always been careful to stay away from roads and villages. He'd never gone by car.

He was still in here by himself, for whatever that was worth. He'd thought Kyrylo would be with him by now. When Solovey had said *both of them*, he must not have meant both of them at the same time.

Or maybe he'd just changed his mind.

For some reason, knowing you were going to get a bullet in your head very soon didn't seem as bad as knowing you were going to be alone when it happened. Even Kyrylo would be better than nobody.

Stupid. What difference did it make? A bullet in the head was a bullet in the head.

He just hadn't wanted to die so far from home. That was what made it hard.

He tried to think about the farm. He tried to picture it there in the darkness under the coat—not the farm the last time he'd seen it, two and a half years ago, right after the Germans took Lyudya, but the farm before the war. It had been a good summer, that last summer, the summer of 1939—or it was a good summer in his memory anyway, but maybe that was just because it had been so comparatively better than all the summers since. There had been some disagreement about whether he would go back to school that term or stay home to help Papa around the farm. Mama had wanted him home. Boys of twelve—farm boys like him—didn't have any more use for schooling. He wasn't meant for university. He wasn't Kyrylo Romaniuk with a rich Canadian uncle. He was Kostyantyn Lasko, meant to work this land the way Laskos had worked this land for three hundred years. It was a poor name but a good one, Lasko—a good farmer's name. He could read, he could write, he could count. What else could school teach him that he needed to know?

Times were changing, Papa said. Poland was changing. Nowadays, even Laskos could go to university if they wanted to.

With whose money? Mama challenged him.

Kostya had met Lyudya's eyes across the table. Nobody else but Kostya knew that Lyudya was saving money for university under her mattress. Nobody else but Kostya knew that was really why she'd taken the position with the Nowaks in the big house across the river, in the Polish part of town—six days a week cooking and cleaning and minding the baby. She got up early to do her farm chores first, and she came home after supper each night, bone-tired. It was all right, she said to Kostya. Just a couple more years. Then she would have enough money saved for the tuition and her room in L'viv and the books for her classes. She was going to be a chemist like Marie Curie. Just a couple of more years. Wait and see.

That was August 1939.

It was stupid in retrospect, talking like that—school or no school, university or no university.

The invasions came in September—Germans sweeping across Poland from the west, Soviets from the east. By October, Papa was dead. He went to a meeting called by the new Soviet author-ities, he and all the other smallholders of the village, and he never came back. At first, people said they'd shipped them off east, off to the labor camps the way they'd done with the army and police, but Karol Nowak had found the bodies in the wood one day when he was out hunting. He made the mistake of telling people, and also of hunting without permission, so the Reds shot him too. But at least then people knew.

The Germans took over two years later, June 1941. There was no question for Kostya by then. Papa was dead. Kostya was staying on the farm. But it still hurt like a fist to his own gut to see Lyudya coming in white-faced from the post office with the bulletin clenched in her trembling hand: All secondary schools and universities were closed to ethnic Slavs, *Untermenschen* like her—serfs of the German Reich. From now on, Poles and Ukrainians need learn only to write their own names and to count to five hundred.

She'd still had the money under her mattress. She'd still been hoping.

And Mama had known, somehow, because she wouldn't take the money when Lyudya tried to give it to her.

"Keep it," she said. "The Nazis won't be here forever."

So the money had still been under her mattress when they took her.

Kostya had left the next day—run off to L'viv trying to find her, like an idiot. Hadn't even left a note. Hadn't seen Mama or Lesya or the farm since that morning.

Hadn't ever found Lyudya either.

He wished he'd left a note. Why hadn't he left a note?

The car was stopping.

He heard the engine cut off and their doors slam. His door opened—the door by his head. Somebody pulled the coat off him.

"Good morning," Solovey said. "Have a nice ride?"

They were in a wide, grassy clearing below a pine wood. There was a white clay farmhouse and a few outbuildings and garden beds not far off—a safe house? Their headquarters?

Andriy was talking to somebody over at the kitchen stoop, silhouetted against soft lamplight. "Morning" was a generous term. It was midnight or a little past. Night mist snaked along the grass and coiled in the hollows. There was no moon, but the stars were out, bright and hard in a wide, clear sky. There were nightingales singing up in the wood.

It wasn't a bad place to die, really.

Solovey pulled Kostya out of the car. He unknotted the gag from Kostya's mouth and opened the handcuffs at Kostya's wrists. Then he steered Kostya around and shoved him toward the house. "Go that way."

Kostya spun back around, stupidly furious. "Look me in the face, coward."

Solovey put his hands on Kostya's upper arms and moved him effortlessly aside so he could open the trunk of the car. "Do you mind?"

Andriy came back across the yard.

"She says put the car in the barn," he said.

Solovey was rummaging in the trunk, slinging musette bags over his shoulder. "Did you tell her about my hot date back in L'viv?"

"She says find a better excuse."

Solovey let out a breath of a laugh. He shouldered another bag.

"She says she waited supper," Andriy said.

"*That's* a coercive measure. That's not fair." Solovey slammed the trunk lid shut. He came up face-to-face with Kostya. "Hello—it's you. Why are you still here?"

Kostya realized his mouth was hanging open. He snapped it shut.

Solovey adjusted his bags.

"You can come in and have supper," he said, "or you can keep standing there looking like a confused salmon. *I* don't care."

Kostya went.

"This is Kostya," Solovey told the tall, elegantly coiffed blond woman at the kitchen stoop. "You can see him under the blood if you look hard enough."

It sounded wrong for some reason—"this is Kostya"—and it took Kostya a stupidly long moment to realize that was because Solovey had said Kostya, not Valerik.

Solovey had already vanished through the doorway. Kostya hung back on the step. The blond woman reached a hand to his elbow and pulled him in, gently but firmly. She leaned close to inspect him in the half-light, pressing fingers gingerly here and there over his face. Her touch stung like needles. Kostya flinched.

She let out a long breath. She pushed him after Solovey. "Go. Sit."

Solovey was at the dining room table, lighting a cigarette, a newspaper spread open in front of him. The blond woman was still in the kitchen, opening and closing cupboards. Kostya sat down stiffly on the edge of a chair, across the table from Solovey.

"How did you know my name?"

Solovey glanced up. "Lucky guess."

"I never told Marko my name."

Solovey flicked his lighter shut and returned it to his breast pocket. "How'd he know Kyrylo is your cousin? How'd he know about your mother and sister in Bród?"

Kostya didn't say anything.

"Marko's an idiot, but he's an idiot with resources. The good news for you is the Reds just got to town, and he's got a treacherous executive officer on his hands. He's a little distracted." Solovey took a thoughtful drag and turned the page of his newspaper. "Kyrylo's the one you've really got to worry about. I wouldn't count on Marko taking care of that problem for you. Wouldn't be surprised"—he exhaled a soft cloud of smoke— "if Kyrylo happened to have some other rat on Marko's staff, you know? Wouldn't be surprised if he already knew to go to ground." He turned another page. "If I were you, I'd be legging it home to Mama and Lesya as fast as I could. And then I'd be packing up and heading for the hills."

Kostya swallowed. His stomach was tight—anger and suspicion and the urgent need to *run* all coiled up in slippery knots. He clenched his hands into fists under the table. He had to stay calm. He had to think. "If you're Kyrylo's rat, why did you get me out?"

Solovey affected a look of wounded innocence. "I didn't say it was *me*."

"I'm not stupid."

"Not much of a cardplayer either, are you?" Solovey flicked the ash from the tip of his cigarette and turned another page. "Coming in looking guilty as hell with that stupid story about a patrol. Trying so very hard to stick to it while Marko bashed your teeth in. I admire the effort."

Kostya looked away. "Where are we?"

"Outside Zarudce—north of L'viv. A friend's. She'll fix you up." Solovey took out his cigarette and studied it absently. "There's something you should probably know before you say anything stup—"

The blond woman came in from the kitchen with a nurse's bag. Solovey gave her a brilliant grin.

"Before we get down to business," he amended smoothly. "This is Mrs. Kijek, by the way."

She was Polish.

Kostya whipped a glance at Solovey, who returned it levelly. Mrs. Kijek took his chin in her fingers and turned his head back.

"Hold still," she said.

She was Polish.

She was the enemy.

He was still wearing his stolen Red uniform. His spare set of clothes—his only set of civilian clothes—was still hanging on the line in his room at the safe house. Solovey was in a UPA uniform. So was Andriy, who was coming in from putting the car in the barn, rifle slung across his back.

You could maybe explain one or the other without her getting suspicious—the Red uniform or the UPA uniforms. You couldn't explain both together.

Mrs. Kijek wasn't asking for explanations. She didn't seem to care.

Nobody seemed to care.

Solovey stuck his cigarette back in his mouth. He nodded at Kostya.

"He needs civilian clothes," he said to Mrs. Kijek.

Mrs. Kijek held Kostya's chin in her fingers and dabbed at his face with a wad of iodine-soaked gauze. "Identification?"

"Do you have identification?" Solovey asked Kostya.

Still bewildered, Kostya blinked. "You mean fake?"

"Ideally."

"I mean—I've got my military card. My Soviet card."

"What about your *Kennkarte*?"

The *Kennkarte* had been his German-issued identification—also fake. Kostya shook his head. "Not with me."

"Lose the military card," Solovey said. "Easier to explain why you haven't got identification than why you've got one of those."

"Money?" Mrs. Kijek asked, peeling an adhesive strip and taping it carefully over Kostya's cheekbone.

"Marks, if you've got them," Solovey said. "He just escaped a German labor camp. If he's going to be carrying money, make it German money." He flicked the ash from his cigarette. "He'll need a gun—preferably a handgun. And a map." He opened his breast pocket, took out a stack of small black-and-white photographs, and leaned forward to slide the photographs across the table to Mrs. Kijek. "Payment," he said.

Mrs. Kijek's hands fell still just for a second.

"It's all there," Solovey said. "Station, train yard, street. Guard postings—as many as I could get. Everything you need."

Mrs. Kijek pressed a cold compress into Kostya's hand. "Hold that."

"She means against your face," Solovey said.

Mrs. Kijek reached for the photographs. Her fingertips brushed over them hesitantly, as though she couldn't quite believe them. "How did you—"

"Very carefully," Solovey said.

"These are from this afternoon."

"Well—except for the shots of the interior. Those are just for reference. Couldn't get in there, obviously. The Hundredth Rifles is using the main hall for barracks. They're keeping prisoners on the first floor—where the offices used to be."

"I can't take these."

"Give them to Jerzy. He's not going to ask questions."

"He was arrested in the city this morning," Mrs. Kijek said.

Solovey swore under his breath. "NKVD?"

"I don't know. We're trying to find out."

"Who does that leave in command?"

Mrs. Kijek hesitated. "Lena."

"Give them to her. Tell her they came from Anna. She's not going to care where Anna got them."

"Is Anna with you?"

"Back at camp."

Mrs. Kijek's voice was suddenly very quiet. "Are you—"

"Keeping myself busy," Solovey said lightly. He gave her a quick, sharp look.

Something wordless passed between them in that look; Kostya could feel it. Mrs. Kijek wiped her hands on her apron and pushed her chair back. Her face was perfectly blank.

"Very well," she said.

"I can ask her to drop by if you think it will lend credibility." Solovey nudged one of the musette bags with the toe of his boot. "These are from her, by the way. The usual—though she wanted to make sure you saw these." He disappeared under the edge of the table while he opened one of the bags. "Morphine packs— American. They came with the Red Cross shipment." He reemerged with a little plastic vial, holding it up triumphantly to show Mrs. Kijek. "What do you think? Enough for a change of clothes and a gun?"

Mrs. Kijek picked up the photographs and bent to kiss him gently on the cheek. "And a map."

"And a map—and a compass."

"I'll see what I can do," Mrs. Kijek said. "Set the table."

* * *

"So what are you?" Kostya asked. "A double agent?"

"That's rich coming from you, rat," Solovey said.

He was setting the dishes on the counter as he washed them. Andriy was asleep on the sofa out in the drawing room, so Kostya was the one stumbling around in the half-light, towel in hand, opening cupboards and hutches, trying to figure out where everything went. He had never seen so many cupboards. The kitchen was the size of Dima and Yuliya's whole apartment. The backed-up pile of washed dishes on the counter was growing precariously large.

"Is *she* a double agent?" he asked.

"Mrs. Kijek? I've never thought about it like that." Solovey shut off the sink tap. He was silent for a moment, apparently thinking about it. "I don't think that's a fair characterization. She's just a genuinely decent person. She would patch up a Red or a German the same way she patched you up. God knows she's patched *me* up a hundred times." He turned the tap back on. "We've got an understanding. I keep her in medicine, she keeps me in newspapers and cigarettes. We share intelligence—within certain parameters, obviously."

Kostya folded his towel over to the marginally drier side. "Photographs of the train station?"

"She has an academic interest in Art Nouveau architecture from the late Hapsburg period."

"I know about the prisoners there." The Reds had started disarming and arresting every Polish Resistance fighter they could get their hands on as soon as they entered the city this morning. They were keeping the prisoners at the station until they could get the rail lines repaired. Then, Kostya assumed, they would be shipping them east. Marko said that was what you got for trying to cut deals with the Soviet leadership.

Marko could laugh now, Kyrylo said. He wouldn't be laughing in a month. When the Reds were done with the Resistance, they would start on the UPA.

Kostya focused intently on the inside of the last soup bowl. "The photos were from this afternoon—before you even knew you'd need *payment* for me. You were just going to give them to her anyway."

"Is that a question?"

Kostya turned the bowl over and dried the back for the third time.

"Pretty sure that's already dry," Solovey said. "See—this is why you've got a backlog, Lasko. You've got to keep it moving. *Labor productivity.* Haven't the Reds taught you anything?"

"Is it true—that story about you shooting those Polish prisoners?" Kostya didn't dare look up from the bowl. "Or is it just something you let people believe so they don't figure out . . ." *That you're consorting with the enemy?* He flapped a hand inarticulately. "This?"

Solovey didn't say anything. The tap kept running this time.

Maybe he hadn't heard. Kostya risked a glance. Solovey's hands moved very deliberately, turning a plate carefully back and forth under the stream of water. His face had gone to stone.

Mrs. Kijek came in from the hall.

"Decide between yourselves," she announced. "The attic bed or the armchair in the study."

"Option three," Solovey said. His voice was level, as if nothing had happened. Maybe nothing *had*—Kostya didn't know. "Push Andriy off the sofa. That's a fun game."

Mrs. Kijek took the plate from him. "Move."

"Too late," Solovey said. "That's the last one." He reached past her to shut off the tap. He didn't look at Kostya. "Actually, we've got to get back—Andriy and me. I wasn't kidding about that date. It's with my commander, but still. He's the jealous sort. Doesn't like me out of his sight too long. Then again, who does?"

Mrs. Kijek said, "Don't you think—"

"Not past midnight."

Mrs. Kijek didn't smile. "Leave the car, Aleksey."

"We'll be careful," Solovey said. "We've got some NKVD stuff we can put on. We look like serious business, believe me. Bet we could walk right into that station without anybody looking at us twice."

Mrs. Kijek took the towel from Kostya and gave him a quick, cool smile. "I'll finish up, dear, thank you." She caught Solovey's eye. "Show him the attic."

Kostya followed Solovey up the narrow, creaking stairs,

tongue tied. *Idiot*—why had he even asked? What the hell had he expected Solovey to say? *Yes, I'm a murderer; no, I'm a traitor.* There was no good answer to the question. Why couldn't he have just kept his mouth shut?

Solovey leaned against the wall at the top of the stairs and lit another cigarette. He waved a vague hand. "Bed, washstand. Linens in the cabinet. The window opens onto the roof if you need to make a quick getaway—and yes, it *has* happened, before you ask."

Kostya's face heated. "I'm sorry."

Solovey put his lighter away.

"Stay away from roads, villages, farms. Cross-country only. Mrs. Kijek will mark a route on the map for you. Stick to it, even if you think it's taking too long. If the Poles or the Reds pick you up, there's no point to any of this."

"I know."

"They weren't prisoners," Solovey said, "just so you know. I set up a meeting. Told them I wanted to talk terms for a cease-fire." He pulled on his cigarette absently. "If it makes you feel any better, they didn't mean it any more than I did. I just happened to have them outgunned."

Kostya gritted his teeth. "You don't have to—"

"Explain myself? To a private? Thank you."

"Look, I shouldn't have asked. It was stupid. I'm sorry."

Solovey pulled on his cigarette and let out a long, smoky breath. "So—if we're being fair—I get to ask you a stupid question."

"Fine."

"Have you ever lost anybody, Kostya? Anybody close to you—as in you still lie awake at night wishing to God it could have been you, not them?"

Kostya looked away. His throat was tight.

Oh, Lyudya—it should have been me.

"Yes," he said.

"Then you're right. I don't have to explain anything to you." Solovey's voice was quiet. "I hope you make it home, Kostya."

5
MARIA

BRÓD, POLAND
TUESDAY, AUGUST 1, 1944

I TOLD PEOPLE I NEVER ONCE IN MY LIFE SET FOOT
outside our village, Bród, until the Germans took me, but that
wasn't technically true. I used to go exploring all over the river
valley with my brother, Tomek, when we were kids.

Bród sat like a lonely little island in a sea of dense, dark forest.
The Słonówka River cut the village in two right up the middle.
Our half, the western half, was Bliższy Bród, Nearer Bród, and
the eastern half, across the river, was Dalszy Bród, Farther Bród—
simple and sensible, like the people who lived there. A paved road
in Dalszy Bród ran north and east to Dubno, the county seat. There
was no road at all on the western bank, just a wagon track with a
bridge going across to Dalszy Bród. Both invading armies, Soviet
and German, had come to Bród from the east, from the paved

road. From the west, from the wood, the only way to find Bród, if you didn't already know, was to stumble upon it by accident.

Mama used to warn us about getting lost. I was never afraid of getting lost. How could I be? The wood was *ours*, Tomek's and mine, like our own little kingdom—almost literally. Kamiński was an old and noble name, and even in our new, democratic Poland the villagers had come asking Papa's permission to hunt and trap in the wood. Even Karol Nowak, whose father was the doctor and the richest man in Bród, came asking permission. Tomek and I never had to ask anybody's permission, and we never got lost. Tomek was the one who showed me all the tricks—how to measure distance using just the position of the sun, how to tell direction without a compass, how to find the likeliest places for water. He had always wanted so badly to be a Scout, but there hadn't been a chapter in Bród, and it was too far to Radziwiłłów. He had taught himself, and then—happy to have an easily impressed audience, I suppose—he taught me.

Even after two and a half years, even after everything, I knew this wood—the way your fingers remember piano keys even after you've been years out of practice. You start, and it comes back. You don't think it will, but it does.

Anyway, I wasn't worrying half so much about getting lost as about being *found*.

I had already run into three different NKVD patrols since I left the Lwów road yesterday morning. This was the fourth. The officer, a scowling comrade lieutenant, clenched my sealed pass and stared at it as if he could will it away with a look. He didn't speak Polish, and he either didn't understand my broken Russian or was pretending not to. One of his men, a blond-headed kid not much older than I was, translated for us haltingly.

The lieutenant shook his head.

"Go back," he said.

"That pass is signed by Comrade Colonel Fyodor Volkov." I was used to arguing with them by now. So far, none of them had pushed back very hard. Volkov's name cowed them into submission pretty quickly. "I've got his personal permission to travel to Bród."

The blond kid started to translate. The lieutenant cut him off. Two words—"*Bród net.*"

There is no Bród.

None of the others had heard of it either. It wasn't on their maps. To be fair, it wasn't on most of *our* maps. At this point, the others had just shrugged, rolled their eyes, and given me back my pass—*Just get out of my way.* This lieutenant was still clenching the paper as if he were this close to just ripping it to pieces.

"There is no Bród," he repeated. "Go back to Lwów."

"Comrade Colonel Volkov—"

"Is not here." He'd dropped the act. He obviously understood me perfectly well. The blond kid retreated to a safe distance.

"All right." I was halfway between frustration and panic—the point at which I usually said something stupid. "I'll go back to

Lwów and tell him *you* decided his orders didn't matter since he's not *here*. What's your name?"

He scowled at me. I scowled back, chin up.

He crumpled the pass in his fist, dropped it at my feet, and shoved past me without another word.

I knelt to pick it up, smoothing it out across my lap—slowly and deliberately, to hide the way my hands were shaking. Oh, that was stupid, stupid. I had to be more careful. I had been relying too much on this pass. I hadn't even thought about what might happen if one of Volkov's own men decided he just didn't care, decided *There is no Bród*, decided I was a Resistance spy. The pass was just a piece of paper.

Comrade Colonel Volkov is not here.

It was another hour before my hands stopped shaking.

* * *

All the run-ins with the NKVD had slowed me down. It was already deep twilight by the time I came out of the wood into our cornfield at the southwestern edge of the village. I should have stopped a while ago. I should have stopped when the light first started to fade. It was stupid, really, to walk in this wood at night—especially alone, without a compass, on a night with no moon and an overcast sky—no matter how well I thought I knew the way. But I was so close, *so close*, and I kept thinking I would be able to see the village lights if I went just a little farther. I kept thinking I had just misremembered the distances.

Our house was the first house you came to, entering Bród from the west. The cornfield sloped up away from the wood, and our house sat at the very top of the rise, facing the river, the rest of the village spread out on the riverbank below. Kamiński, as I said, was an old and noble name; our house had been built as a lord's house, on the high ground on the outskirts of the village. You could see all of Bliższy Bród from our front yard.

I hadn't misremembered.

The house wasn't here.

The village wasn't here.

There were traces like fading scars—crumbled walls, burned-out shells of houses. Scattered piles of cracked, blackened chimney stones and charred rafters. Ruts and gashes here and there in the long yellow grass.

There is no Bród.

There hadn't been for a long time either, judging by the overgrowth—except somebody had obviously been tending the graves here in the yard.

There were two graves—two plain, weathered white crosses, one next to the other. No names, no dates, no reasons. I knew whose they were. I think I had been bracing myself to find them ever since I heard that warning in Comrade Colonel F. Volkov's voice.

Two and a half years was too long. I had come back too late.

Oh, Mama, oh, Papa—I'm sorry.

I dropped to my knees beside the near cross, exhausted. I had taught myself to do this—to take the grief and turn it into physical sensation. I had taught myself to do it after Tomek died, and I honed the skill over weeks and months and years in the Opel plant. If you could make the grief merely physical, you could train yourself to ignore it, the way you learned eventually to ignore aching muscles and blistered fingers—or you could allow yourself to believe there was some cure, some objective fix. I dropped to my knees because I was tired, absolutely bone-tired. I needed sleep; that was it.

Somebody had been making an effort to keep the weeds trimmed back from the crosses. There was something unsettling about it—the careful tidiness of the graves in the middle of all this rubble and ruin. I hadn't heard a sound or seen a movement since I came out of the wood, just the wind in the grass and the distant calls of the nightingales, but sitting here by the neatly tended graves in the half-light, I had the stupid, shivery feeling there was somebody else here, somebody else watching.

I didn't want to spend the night here.

I didn't really have a choice. Where else was there to go? Perhaps there were survivors across the river in Dalszy Bród—somebody, *anybody* who could tell me what had happened—but it was another half-hour walk to get across the river. I didn't want to risk it in the dark. There was no telling who or what I would find. I didn't want to risk stumbling into another NKVD patrol. I had run too many risks in the last few days.

No—better to wait for daylight.

Our stock barn was still here—the one thing in all of Bliższy Bród left standing. It was a monstrous old stone castle of a barn, probably older than the house. Somebody had *tried* to burn it. The doors were off, and you could see soot on the walls where they had set the hay on fire in the loft. The flames must not have gone high enough to catch the wooden rafters. The roof itself was slate tile, not thatch—stubbornly indestructible.

I had the Walther, and from the hayloft windows, which went all the way around the barn, I had a good bird's-eye view of the fields to the eaves of the wood. There was some old feed sacking for blankets, and enough dusty hay left to pile into a decent bed—just for a few hours, just until I had enough light to follow the track to Dalszy Bród.

This was another trick I taught myself after Tomek died. I made plans—comfortable, manageable little plans. I focused on little things, practical things, things I knew I could control. One step, then another. It worked if I kept myself busy enough—if I didn't stop taking those steps. If I didn't stop to *think*. Busyness was my ally. Stillness and silence were the enemy.

It was a war I was never going to win, of course. Sooner or later, you had to stop. Sooner or later, there were no more steps, no more tricks, no more plans.

It was a war of attrition. All the enemy had to do was wait you out.

Tonight, at last, they waited me out.

Memories came spilling into the cracks and breaches of my mind. Good memories to start: long summer days in the wood with Tomek, pretending we were knights questing for the top of the Glass Mountain; and crisp, cold winter nights, candle-light and frost glistening on the windowpanes, and the sweet, sharp smell of poppy-seed rolls and gingerbread and fresh-cut pine greenery; and that early autumn afternoon—September 6, 1939, the day Kraków fell, the day before Tomek left, the last day we were all together, the last day of that old life before the world fell apart—when the oak trees were just starting to turn to gold and Karol Nowak kissed me behind the schoolhouse.

And then the other memories, unstoppable as tanks.

The envelope in Mama's hand—the letter from the Ministry of Military Affairs that said Tomek was never coming home. She had always been so strong, my mama, but she wasn't strong enough for that. She hadn't even opened it, just stood there holding it, white-faced, murmuring a soundless little prayer; finally Papa had to ease it from her fingers and open it. Long lines of prisoners on the Dubno road—our own soldiers first, in the weeks and months after the Soviet invasion, then later haggard, stumbling Soviet prisoners being marched west after the Germans swept through. Karol Nowak dead in the snow on the square, a Soviet commissar's bullet in his head; it hadn't been quite three months since he kissed me. That morning, that dreadful morning, February 23, 1942—the pounding on the door, the clipped orders in German, the cargo truck coughing exhaust in the yard. The stupid, stupid lie that had slipped out of my mouth. *I'll come back*, I said. *I'll be back tonight.* I hadn't said goodbye. I hadn't wanted to believe that was goodbye—but I knew, didn't I? Looking back now, it was impossible to think I hadn't known. I must have known. They must have known I would never come back. Why hadn't I said goodbye? It was too late to say it now.

I buried my face in the sacking, slipped my arms around my knees, and cried myself quietly to sleep in the dark.

* * *

It was still dark when I woke up.

It was late, not early. The nightingales were still singing. I had only been asleep for a little while.

There were voices in the barnyard. That was what had woken me up—voices, booted footsteps. Somebody was flashing an electric torch.

Another NKVD patrol. Why were there so many?

I fumbled in my coat pocket for my pass. Should I call down that I was here, or should I just wait and let them find me? Right now, either way seemed like a good way to get shot. Everybody was trigger-happy in the dark.

I didn't trust the pass quite as much after this morning. I crouched under the sacking, pass in one hand and pistol in the other. They were probably just making the rounds anyway—a routine check. I doubted they would bother coming up into the loft.

The torch shone in from the doorway, the beam darting around the empty stalls below me. I watched through the floor grating as they filed in—three of them, in the NKVD olive drab. My heart sank. *No.* They were taking off their packs, unslinging their rifles. They were getting ready to spend the night.

Two more soldiers came in from the yard, hauling a wounded comrade between them. Their lieutenant followed, pistol in hand.

No—not a wounded comrade. He was in civilian clothes.

A prisoner.

They shoved him up against one of the stall doorposts, jerked his arms up behind the post, and tied his wrists. He was a peasant boy about my age, tall and slim, with a short, uneven crop of sun-streaked brown hair and a farmer's tan. Somebody else had been roughing him up lately. Ugly bruises were just starting to fade around his mouth, across his cheekbones. There was a scab crusted on his upper lip.

Without a word, the lieutenant snapped the action of his pistol, took lazy aim, and blew apart the boy's left kneecap.

I gasped, stupidly, and scrambled to stifle my mouth with wadded handfuls of sacking. Nobody heard me over the boy's strangled sob. Nobody looked up. None of the soldiers were really even paying attention. Two of them were busy building a cook fire just outside the doorway. The others were rummaging in their packs, unscrewing canteens, passing around cigarettes. I curled up against the wall, swallowing my own sob.

The lieutenant holstered his pistol.

"I've found it saves time," he said, "starting with that."

He opened his breast pocket and took out a cigarette case. He selected a cigarette, tapped it smoothly against the case, and dipped his head to light it. His face was obscured briefly in a cloud of smoke. He slipped the case back into his pocket and looked back up at the shivering boy.

"I know you think it doesn't make much difference whether you talk because we're going to hang you anyway, so let me explain." He flicked ash from his cigarette into the boy's face. "No—look at me," he said.

The boy's eyes were squeezed shut, his jaw clenched. His chalk-white, sweating face was screwed up with the effort of not making noise. The lieutenant leaned close.

"Look at me," he said softly, "or you get it in the other one."

The boy looked. Tears trembled at the corners of his eyes.

"You decide to talk, you're the only one who hangs. You decide to keep your mouth shut, your family hang with you." The lieutenant shrugged. "There. Not too hard, is it?"

"Don't have any family." The boy gritted it out through shut teeth.

"You said you were going home to Bród. Was that a lie?"

"Bród's home. Doesn't m-mean I've got family there."

"I guess we'll find out," the lieutenant said, "tomorrow on the scaffold. They're going to watch, you know—the whole village. They're all going to get to see what we do with fascists like you."

"I'm not a fascist." The boy's voice was low and furious.

"Tell that to *these* people." The lieutenant waved a vague hand around the barn. He flicked more ash into the boy's face. "Tell me about your mission."

"Already told you. I'm not UPA."

"And I already told you what would happen if you didn't start talking." The lieutenant blew a soft, smoky breath. "Your family are going to hang with you tomorrow, fascist. Now you're just saving yourself some pain."

"I'm not UPA."

"You're a UPA spy. What was your mission in Bród?"

"I'm not UPA."

"Where did you get the map? The map with Soviet troop positions marked on it?"

The boy didn't say anything.

The lieutenant touched the tip of his cigarette to the boy's collarbone. "Where did you get the map?"

Silence.

The lieutenant put his cigarette back in his mouth and took his pistol back out. He snapped the action and aimed at the boy's other knee.

"One more chance," he said.

I shot him.

Something snapped inside of me, the pistol flew up, my finger pulled the trigger—*crack*—and the lieutenant dropped, all in the space of a heartbeat. I didn't think about it.

If I had thought about it, I wouldn't have done it.

There were five more of them, but that wasn't the hard part. I had very good aim. I had always had very good aim. Tomek could tell you. He taught me, and he always said I had better aim than he did. And I had rounds and time to spare. My Walther pistol took an eight-round clip, and none of them had their rifles ready. And I had killed men before. I was thirteen years old the first time I shot to kill. A pair of German scouts had found me when I was out leaving food for the Resistance squad in the wood that first winter after the German invasion. There were only the two of them, and they hadn't wanted to haul a prisoner all the way back to the village, so they were just going to shoot me. I was just a girl; they hadn't bothered searching me for weapons first.

I shot them with Papa's Nagant revolver from the first war. I was sick afterward—all the rest of the day. I told Mama and Papa it was because I had found some bodies in the wood. I never told them the truth. I never told anybody, not even in a confessional. Who was there to confess to? The Soviets had deported our priest, Father Piotr, in April 1940. But I wasn't sorry for it. I had never been sorry for it.

I had never killed men like this, though—one after another,

from a concealed position, before they even had the chance to fight back.

I had never felt like an executioner before.

The fourth man took two shots; by then my hand was shaking. The last one got away. I wasted a bullet on him. He slipped out into the dark, and my bullet glanced uselessly off the doorpost behind him. He didn't take his rifle: There were five rifles still scattered among the bodies on the barn floor. He was off to raise the alarm.

I kept the Walther out as I came down the loft ladder, but none of the bodies were moving. The boy watched me warily. His ragged breaths were loud in the silence. His hands were clenched in trembling fists behind the post. His knee was a shredded, bloody mess.

"*Wszystko w porządku,*" I said in Polish. It's all right. They had been using Russian, the boy and the lieutenant, but the boy's Russian wasn't native. I could tell because it sounded like mine. I stepped closer, slowly. My throat was tight. "I'm a friend, all right? I'm not going to hurt you."

"Resistance?" His Polish wasn't native either. He was still on his guard, chin up. There was fear in the question.

The lieutenant had called him *fashist*. Fascist, Nazi.

Oh, God help me—had I just rescued a Nazi?

His eyes were on the pistol in my hand. He saw my fingers tighten reflexively on the grip. His breath hitched. Just for a second, there was sheer panic in his face. His bound wrists jerked against the post.

Then he went very still.

I made up my mind all at once. I slid the pistol into my coat pocket and showed him my empty hands.

"I'm not Resistance. This is my farm, my family's farm. I mean—it was." I swallowed. "I'm Maria—Maria Kamińska. Who are you?"

Slowly, his gaze moved from my hands to my face. He had startling eyes—bright, piercing blue, the exact color of cornflowers.

His shoulders loosened just a little. "K-Kostya."

He must be Ukrainian.

It made sense. There were Ukrainians across the river in Dalszy Bród—or there had been last I knew. There weren't any here in Bliższy Bród since the pacification. Back in the thirties, some Ukrainian terrorists had burned a couple of Polish farms and blown up some rail lines outside Lwów, so the government sent in the police and army to go through the villages and search all the Ukrainian houses for weapons and explosives. I was too young to remember any of it, but Tomek wasn't. In Bliższy Bród, the pacification had turned violent. Two police officers had been killed. The police had burned down every Ukrainian house on this side of the river in reprisal and sent every adult male to the prison camp at Bereza Kartuska.

"Serves them right," Tomek told me superiorly later. He was eleven years old by then, almost a grown-up to my seven-year-old self, and we were playing in one of the burned-out ruins. "They're all terrorists and traitors."

He was just repeating what he had heard Papa say. Papa was a true Polish patriot. He was always talking like that about Ukrainians and Reds. Mama wouldn't ever contradict him outright, but sometimes when Papa wasn't there she would tell Tomek quietly that you couldn't say *all*. Her older sister, Maria—the Maria I was named for, though I don't think Papa ever realized that—had defied Grandpapa to marry a Ukrainian peasant farmer back in the twenties, before the Soviets closed the border. Mama never said a word against Papa or Grandpapa to their faces. But once a week she went across the river to Dalszy Bród to have our corn milled at the Ukrainian-owned mill there just because, and every year she tried writing our cousin Anatol for his birthday even though Papa said she shouldn't. The letters just came back anyway.

Hesitantly, cautiously, I reached for the boy's hands. He tensed when I touched him.

"It's all right." I tried to sound reassuring—as much for myself as for him. My heart was pounding. "I'm just going to untie you."

"Good luck," he said.

It took me a second of fumbling with his wrists to understand what he meant. I couldn't see very well. They never got that fire going. The only light was the narrow beam from the electric torch. They must not have had any rope: They tied his wrists with detonating cord. It was knotted so tightly I couldn't dig my fingernails under the loops. I picked at it uselessly, my fingers slippery and shaking.

"I'm sorry, I'm sorry—"

"Try cutting it." His voice was tight.

"I haven't got a knife."

"Bayonet."

"What?"

"Try one of their bayonets."

It was still tricky even with the bayonet—trying to get the long, awkward blade between the loops of cord with enough force to cut the wire but without slicing his wrists open. I think I nicked him when the wire finally snapped and the cord burst free, but he didn't make a sound. He didn't move either. He watched dully, his shoulders braced against the post, his weight off his left leg, his face slick with sweat, while I swooped to unbuckle the dead lieutenant's holster. I snatched up the lieutenant's pistol and rifled quickly through his pockets for spare ammunition.

"Do you know if they've got a first-aid kit?"

The boy's eyes had drifted shut. They snapped back open, refocusing. "What?"

"If they've got a first-aid kit."

"Don't think they were t-too worried about that," he said. "I'm supposed to hang t-tomorrow."

I spent a few fruitless minutes yanking open their packs and dumping stuff on the floor. No medical supplies, not even bandages. The most helpful thing I found was a nearly full bottle of vodka.

"Need to go," the boy said.

"You're not going very far on that knee." I stuffed the bottle, the electric torch, and the spare ammunition into one of the packs. Some random food tins, cigarettes, and matches too—good trade value. I slipped the lieutenant's holster over my head. "We'll have to figure something out." I went back over to pull his arm across my shoulders. "What's with all the NKVD anyway? This is the fifth patrol I've seen since yesterday morning."

He rested his hand on my shoulder lightly, shyly, as if he were afraid he might break me. "They're hunting," he said.

"Hunting what?"

"Resistance. UPA. Everybody."

"What are UPA?" That name again—the other thugs Comrade Colonel F. Volkov had warned me about.

The boy didn't answer. He was trying to match my step in the darkness. His fingers clutched so tightly that I had to bite the inside of my cheek to keep from yelping. He had a very strong grip.

"I'm sorry," he said.

"It's all right."

"I don't know if I can—"

"It's all right. It's just hard because you're taller."

"Oh, this is hard for *you*?" His teeth were gritted.

My face heated. "That's not what I meant."

He let out a low hiss of a breath. "It was a joke. Guess I'm n-not very good at them."

"Not very good at keeping in step either, are you?"

There was a stretch of silence. We were in the cornfield now, hobbling along like contestants in a three-legged race.

Then, out of the darkness somewhere above me, he said, "Was that a joke too?"

"Yes, that was a joke."

"All right," he said.

He went very quiet after that. We were both being quiet, but I could feel the physical effort of his silence. His fingers dug so deep into my shoulder that my arm was numb.

After a while, he said, "I think I've got to stop."

He said it in Ukrainian.

And he slipped to the ground without another word, landing with a soft *thump* in the dead leaves.

He was out cold.

We had come maybe a kilometer from the farm—not very far. I was pretty sure I could still see the edge of our cornfield from here if it were daylight. We had come down a long, low bank onto a spit of weedy flatland. The wood was pretty sparse here—scrubby birch brush and young poplars. Not much good for cover. I rolled the boy over onto his back. For a second, I thought about trying to drag him.

For half a second, I thought about leaving him.

Then I thought about the NKVD finding him after what *I* did to that squad in the barn.

Because they would find him. They would find him, they would torture him, they would kill him—and as much as I could try to convince myself it wasn't really my fault, they were going to kill him anyway, I would always remember I had chosen to leave him.

I couldn't leave him. Like it or not, we were stuck together now.

I slipped the holster and the pack from my shoulder and took out the bottle of vodka. I didn't know very much about treating wounds, but I knew I might as well do this part while he couldn't feel it—while he couldn't scream. I ripped a ribbon of cloth from the hem of my skirt and sat down beside him in the leaves to dress what was left of his knee.

Afterward, I took both pistols and the spare ammunition and went back up the bank to keep watch from the high ground. There wasn't really much point, given—first—that I had already decided I wasn't going to leave him, and—second—that we wouldn't outrun anybody even if I could get him on his feet. But it was something to do.

The night passed very slowly.

I woke up to machine-gun fire.

It was faint and far-off, somewhere east of us. It went on and on like the low growl of thunder in a summer storm. There were short, intermittent pauses where the gunner must have been reloading. Then it picked up again.

It went on for what must have been ten minutes.

Then it stopped—just like that.

It was just now dawn. Streaks of pale pink light were shooting up over the trees. I felt stupid for falling asleep even if there wasn't any point keeping watch in the first place. I had gotten sloppy lately. I had been sloppy since Lwów.

The gunfire made me nervous—the way it went on and on and then just stopped.

Time to get out of here.

I slid down the bank and crossed back over to where the boy was lying sprawled limply in the leaves. His eyes were shut and sunken. His face was ashy-pale under the bruises. My terrible makeshift bandage on his knee was soaked through with blood.

It occurred to me he could be dead.

He *looked* dead.

I had sat here all night, and he could have been dead the whole time.

I crouched slowly beside him, heart in my throat, and slipped my fingers under his jaw to feel the pulse.

He lurched awake with a hissed breath, eyes flying open. One hand closed like a vise on my wrist, yanking my hand away. The other slid over my throat.

"I'm sorry," I gasped, "I'm sorry, I was just—I thought—"

"Resistance?" His voice was furious.

"I'm not Resistance." Oh God—his grip was tight, so tight. "Don't you remember? I'm Maria—Maria Kamińska." Stupidly, I couldn't remember his name. Kesya? Kolya? I couldn't think. I couldn't breathe. "I saved your life last night, you id—"

He let me go as if I had burned him. He dropped back against the leaves, stunned and blinking, arms flung wide.

"I'm sorry," he said.

I backed hastily away from him, rubbing my throat with numb fingers. My heart was pounding. "You don't remember?" It didn't come out as primly as I would have liked. I sounded hoarse, breathless. I sounded scared.

I was scared. His fingers were still around my neck. His hands were crawling all over me. Shame flushed across my skin. I shuddered and pulled my coat tighter, hunching my shoulders, making myself small.

He looked away.

"Yeah," he said. "I'm sorry."

Then he said almost shyly, "What were you doing?"

I drew a long, steadying breath. He wasn't touching me. Nobody was touching me. *Focus, Maria. One step, then another.* "Checking your pulse. You were passed out all night. I thought you were dead."

"I woke up a few times," he said. "I just didn't move. Didn't really know where I was so there wasn't much point. Didn't know you were still here."

"I was up there—keeping watch." I wasn't going to tell him I fell asleep.

He still wasn't looking at me. "Did I hurt you?"

"Scared me a little," I said too lightly. "That's some reflex."

He didn't say anything.

"Why are you so afraid of the Resistance?"

"I'm not afraid."

"That's the first thing you've asked me—both times. I think you're more worried about the Resistance than you are about the NKVD. What are you, a Nazi collaborator?"

"I'm not a Nazi." He spit it out between shut teeth.

"Then what are you afraid of?"

He didn't say anything. He scowled off across the flatland at an offending poplar tree.

"I think you owe me an explanation," I snapped. "I could have been twenty kilometers away by now if I didn't have to worry about *you*."

It wasn't really fair of me. Twenty kilometers was a pretty generous estimate. I couldn't have gone that far in the dark. But I was angry.

I waited for him to say just as angrily, *Nobody was making you stay, were they?* But he didn't.

"Thank you," he said. "For staying."

It was disarmingly earnest, but I refused to let him off so easily. "That's not an explanation."

He seemed to come to a decision. He braced his shoulders against the ground.

"I lied to them," he said. "When they were interrogating me last night. I lied to them."

"No kidding."

"I'm UPA." He looked back at me quickly—looking for a reaction. "I mean—I'm not anymore, but I was. I fought with L'viv Group. It's a long story."

"I don't know what UPA means."

His brow furrowed. "The Insurgent Army—the Ukrainian Insurgent Army. Ukrainska Povstanska Armiia."

"So when you say you fought . . ." I swallowed. I was pretty sure I didn't want to know the answer to this question. "Who were you fighting?"

"Poles." His voice was quiet. "Poles, Reds, Germans. All of them." The furrow deepened. "How the hell do you not—"

"Look, I don't know anything about what's happened here, all right? The last I knew, this was Bliższy Bród. Now it's just a bunch of weeds. So save it." I yanked open the pack and shoved the spare ammunition back in. My throat was stupidly tight. *A bunch of weeds and my parents' graves.* I wasn't really angry at him, I didn't think, but I was still angry. "So, what—you're some sort of Ukrainian nationalist radical? You blow up railway stations and ransack Polish farms?"

"I don't kill civilians," he said stiffly.

"That's just the other terrorists, is it?"

"I'm not a terrorist. I'm not a nationalist." He was getting angry too. "The Reds killed my father. The Germans kidnapped my sister. What the hell was I supposed to do?"

"Give me a piece of your shirt."

He blinked. "What?"

"Give me a piece of your shirt. I'm going to rewrap your knee, and I haven't got any bandages."

He lay very still and watched, clutching handfuls of weeds and dead leaves, while I gingerly unwrapped my strip of skirt from his knee. Oh, I should have been glad for the dark last night. The knee looked ghastly. The whole kneecap was flopping around loose like an untacked shingle. Pale, pale bone poked up through the skin.

I can't do this. I can't do this.

I had to do this. One step, then another.

I held his knee under one hand and reached for the pack. I fished around awkwardly for the bottle of vodka. It was empty—not a drop left. For a second, I just stared at it stupidly. I knew there was at least a quarter of the bottle left last night. I knew I recapped it.

"Did you—"

"I'm sorry," he said.

"*All* of it?"

"It's just this really hurts."

I sighed and shoved the empty bottle back into the pack.

"I know. But that was the closest thing we had to an antiseptic. This is going to get infected if you don't get real medicine soon." I laced the strip of shirt carefully under his knee, looped it around, and pulled it tight.

He stiffened. He swore in Ukrainian. *"Layno, layno, layno."*

Then he said, in Polish, "You d-don't understand Ukrainian, do you?"

"Just the dirty words."

"I'm sorry."

"It was a joke. You can swear. I don't mind. I've got to do that again, you know."

"Layno."

"Just talk to me." I threaded the ends of the strip under his knee again. "How long since you've been home?"

His fingers were dug into the dirt, white-knuckled. His eyes were squeezed shut. "Two years. Two and a half. I can't remember. Right after they t-took Lyudya."

I pulled the strip tight. "February 1942?"

He sucked a long, shuddering breath. "I—I think."

"That's when they took me."

His eyelids fluttered open. *"Ostarbeiter?"*

"Yes—until last month. The automobile plant in Rüsselsheim."

"Was she with you?"

He had that same sharp, haunted look I remembered on Comrade Colonel F. Volkov's face—half hopeful, half desperate.

I hated it. I *hated* it.

"I don't know," I told him.

"Lyudmyla Vitaliyivna Lasko." He didn't even seem to notice what I was doing to his knee anymore. "She had to have been with you. It would have been the same transport."

I focused on tying off the strip. I couldn't bear to look him in the face. "I don't know."

"Please. She would have been—"

"I don't *know*, all right? I didn't ask names. I didn't make friends. Do you want to know why? Because we never knew who was going to end up shot by the end of the day, or hanged, or bombed to bits. You just kept your head down and your mouth shut." His blood was all over my hands. I wiped my trembling fingers on the leaves. "If your sister's lucky, she's already dead."

He didn't say anything. He didn't make a sound. He had his dirt-stained fingers spread across his face as if to block me out. His shoulders shook.

I shoved the pack up against his elbow and dropped the spare pistol on the leaves beside it. "There. Pistol, ammunition. I'm going to go get help."

"Wait," he said.

He slid his hands down, swallowing. He struggled to sit up, crooking his legs awkwardly. Pain twisted his face.

"Stop—please stop." I winced on his behalf. "What are you doing?"

He fumbled with the tongue of his right boot. "They missed it when they searched me," he said. He held a compass out on a trembling palm. "B-better stay off the road."

I didn't really need a compass in daylight, but I took it to make him happy. It occurred to me only later that he knew I didn't need it in daylight.

He gave it to me because he thought I wasn't coming back.

6
MARIA

THERE WAS SOMETHING BURNING OVER TOWARD
Dalszy Bród.

I didn't see the smoke until the riverbank. I had made a wide
loop around the ruins of Bliższy Bród, keeping to the wood. I
hadn't really had a good, clear look at the sky until now. Thick,
black smoke boiled up over the trees on the far bank. The wind
was whisking it off eastward; that was why I hadn't smelled it.

They were burning off the fields, probably—clearing the soil
for the winter grain crop. They would be ringing the church bells
if it were a building on fire.

The river was slow and shallow enough here in summertime
to cross on foot if you didn't mind a wet skirt hem. Good thing

too—the bridge was out. I hadn't even noticed in the dark last night.

I was still twisting water out of my hem, my stockings and boots off, when somebody said in Polish, "Hands up. Come up here."

A rifleman was watching me from the trees at the top of the bank, rifle shouldered. He was wearing a German infantry coat and helmet, but the armband on his right sleeve was white and red, the colors of the Polish flag—the colors of the Resistance.

I straightened slowly, showing him my hands. He beckoned impatiently with the rifle. "Come up here."

Another rifleman materialized from nowhere out of the trees and fell in behind me as I climbed barefoot up the bank. They had probably been watching the whole time I was in the water. There really wasn't any way to be covert about crossing a river in broad daylight. The fact that they hadn't taken the opportunity to shoot me was promising. At least they seemed to be planning to ask questions first.

The first man kept his rifle trained as I approached.

"Lose the weapon," he ordered.

I dropped my hands to unbuckle my holster strap.

"One hand," he snapped. "Keep the other up."

Awkwardly, I worked the strap loose with one hand and lowered the holster very slowly to the ground.

"Now kick it to me."

I pushed the holster toward him with my bare toes.

He lowered his rifle.

"Go get her shoes," he said to the other man. He slung the rifle and crouched to pick up my pistol, looping the belt on his arm while he checked the magazine. He looked back up.

"Are you hurt?"

"What?"

His face was perfectly blank. "You're bleeding."

I had the Ukrainian boy's blood all over the front of my coat. I shook my head. "No—it's not mine. I, um . . ." Oh, this was a problem. Did I ask for their help? They were bound to find out the boy was UPA. He was in too much pain to think clearly. He had probably already said some things to me he wished he hadn't.

What would they do to him if they found out?

Oh, heaven—the fear and fury in his voice when he asked whether I was Resistance.

"Open your coat," the Resistance soldier ordered.

"I'm not hurt." I fumbled at my coat buttons, fingers slippery. Panic hummed at the back of my mind. *Breathe, Maria.* "I ran into some NKVD last night. I—"

Still had Comrade Colonel F. Volkov's hammer-and-sickle-stamped pass in my lining pocket.

How could I be so stupid? It wasn't going to do me any good after last night—after I let a witness get away. I'd had to lean over the ledge to get those shots off; I had to assume the survivor had seen me. By now, every NKVD unit from here to Tarnopol probably knew to look for the girl with the shaved head. Why hadn't I gotten rid of it?

Resistance thugs won't care that you're a civilian. A pass from me is a death sentence in the wrong hands.

The snowy-white stationery practically jumped out of my drab coat lining. The Resistance soldier held out a hand automatically, one eyebrow quirking. "Identification?"

"I haven't got any." I fought the urge to snap my coat shut again. "I've just escaped a German labor camp. I'm from here— from Bród. I mean—I was. My name is Maria Kamińska."

He was still holding out his hand. "What's that?"

I glanced down stupidly. "You mean—"

"That paper."

"No, it's just"—I gave him a weak little smile—"something personal."

He matched my smile a little viciously. His eyes were cool. He had my pistol turned on me now. "Let's have a look."

There was no way out of it. The second soldier, coming back up from the water with my boots, stepped up right behind me, blocking me in. Numbly, I slid the pass from my coat lining and handed it over. The first soldier flipped it open one-handed, keeping the pistol trained.

His chin came up.

"You've got some friends in high places for a girl from Bród who's just escaped a German labor camp."

"Listen—I can explain."

He folded the paper back up and tucked it in his breast pocket. He motioned with the pistol. "Put your shoes on. You can explain to the commander." He glanced at the other soldier. "I'll take her up. Wait for me."

"Please—just wait. *Wait*." I was desperate now. I didn't have time for this. I had lost half an hour already. It would be mid-morning before I made it back across the river—and that was if they were going to let me go right now, not haul me in front of their commander for an interrogation.

The boy wouldn't last that long.

I had left him to die just as he thought.

Oh God—I had left him that pistol.

Oh, please, God, no—if he thought his only other choice was to lie there waiting for the NKVD to find him again . . .

"Listen—I've got a friend back there." My mouth was dry. "He's hurt pretty badly. I was on my way to Dalszy Bród for help, but I don't think he can wait that long."

The two of them exchanged an odd look over my shoulder.

"Dalszy Bród?" the first soldier said. "Haven't you seen it?"

The coldness in his voice made my heart clench. "Seen what?"

He jerked his chin impatiently. "Just put your shoes on."

"Seen *what*?"

The second soldier, a freckled, bookish-looking boy, handed me my boots one after the other.

"The smoke," he said quietly. "The UPA ambushed an NKVD squad last night. Killed four soldiers and an officer." He scuffed at the dirt with the toe of his boot. "So the NKVD raided Dalszy Bród this morning. Machine-gunned everybody, burned the houses. That's what all that smoke is."

No, no, no.

I fumbled blindly at my boot laces. My hands wouldn't cooperate. "Why?"

"Let's go," the first soldier ordered.

"But—the whole village. Why?"

"*Krugovaya poruka*," the freckled soldier said, stumbling a little over the Russian. "Collective guilt. Some of them were from there, I guess—some of the UPA."

"Serves them right," the first soldier muttered. "Let the *rezuni* get a taste of their own medicine."

It was an ugly slur for Ukrainians—*rezuni*, savages. We used to say it when we play-battled as kids, Tomek and I, reenacting the defense of Lwów against the Ukrainian rebels, until Mama made us stop.

"It wasn't the UPA," I said.

"What?"

"It wasn't the UPA who killed those soldiers." *God have mercy.* I wanted to be sick. "It was me."

They both paused, staring.

"And—and my friend," I added a little weakly. "They stopped us last night in Bliższy Bród. They thought we were Resistance spies. They were going to shoot us." Oh, I had to be careful. "Please. My friend is hurt badly. I need your help."

The first soldier stepped up right into my face—so quickly that I took a reflexive step back.

"Do you know what I think?" he snarled. "I think you're a liar. I think you're a collaborator—a dirty little Red collaborator. I think you'll say anything at all if you think it'll keep us from putting a bullet in your head." His fingers snaked around my elbow. He yanked at my arm. "So you're going to shut up, and you're going to come with me."

"Edek," somebody said.

The voice was familiar—so familiar.

So wrong.

Edek could tug at my arm all he wanted. I couldn't move.

My brother, Tomek, was standing at the top of the bank.

7
MARIA

WE GOT THE NOTICE ABOUT TOMEK FROM THE
Ministry of Military Affairs on September 24, 1939, one week
after the Soviet invasion, not quite three weeks after he had lied
about his age to join the Polish army.

There was a whole letter, but I really only saw two words.

Captured. Executed.

Those early days were full of confusion, misinformation. We
didn't even know the Soviet invasion was an invasion at first.
Honestly, we thought the Soviets had come to help us fight the
Germans. For a few days after the Soviets got here, nothing much
happened. Tomek's infantry unit was just sitting in Równe, waiting for orders.

Then the arrests started.

We pieced the story together later. When the Soviets came to disarm them, Tomek and some of the other soldiers in his unit had tried to resist—to fight their way out. Romania was still neutral then, and a lot of Polish soldiers were heading south, trying to make it out before the borders were sealed—to Romania, then to France, where our government was already being set up in exile. We thought that was probably what Tomek and his mates had been trying to do since the letter said they had been captured three hundred kilometers south of here, near the Romanian border.

Captured, executed—just like that. The letter didn't say how.

Part of me felt as though I had died with him—as though there were a hole where my heart used to be.

Part of me wished I had.

Part of me said, *It's a lie. It's a mistake. It's got to be a mistake. They can't get rid of him so easily—not Tomek Kamiński. Not your big brother, Tomek. He's alive. He's alive. You KNOW he's alive.*

I had spent five years trying to get that part of me to shut up.

* * *

"Tomek," I gasped.

It was stupid, I knew it was stupid—revealing I knew him, revealing his name.

I didn't care.

"But they said—they told us—there was a letter—"

He wrapped his arms around me tightly, so tightly. I don't think I had really realized until that moment, crushed breathless in his hug, what two and a half years in that German factory had done to me physically. He was so strong, so solid, so warm, and I was so small, so cold, so thin and fragile, as if my ribs might just snap and splinter like matches if he squeezed much tighter.

But I didn't want him to stop. I didn't want him ever to stop.

He pressed his lips gently to the shameful stubble on my scalp. They kept our heads shaved in the factory because they didn't want us carrying lice, and my hair still hadn't grown out more than a finger width. A sob pulled at my chest. I couldn't help it. I couldn't stop it. I clutched his coat in handfuls and buried my face in his shoulder, and I cried, and I cried, and I cried.

He rested his chin on top of my head and murmured my name over and over—my familiar name, the only name he ever used for me.

"Maja—Maja—it's all right. It's going to be all right."

Then he said, "Where's your friend?"

And it was as if the spell had broken.

It was all real again, sharply real, hatefully real—the smoke clinging to his coat, the streaks of dirt and ash and sweat on his face, the pistol in his hand. The rest of his squad, eight or ten of them altogether, were coming down the bank, gathering around us in a half circle, curious, uncertain.

And for one stupid, selfish moment, I didn't want to answer him. I didn't want to care. I wanted to forget about that wretched

Ukrainian boy with his wretched knee. I wanted to forget about those five dead NKVD soldiers. I wanted to forget that Dalszy Bród was burning because of me.

I just wanted to keep standing here like this, safe in the circle of his arms, letting him hug away the chill in my bones and the ache in my heart and the guilt in my soul.

Just for a moment—just for once in five long years—I wanted to rest. I wanted to forget about everything and close my eyes and rest.

But instead I heard myself saying levelly, calmly, "I left him in the wood about a kilometer from the farm. I can show you."

Tomek issued orders over my head. "Lew—with me. Bring your kit. Edek, set the perimeter. Rendezvous at the oak in an hour."

Edek's cool eyes lingered on me. "Take Julian, sir. Another gun won't hurt."

"I've got Maja." Tomek squeezed my arm. "She's a better shot than I am."

Oh—the look that flashed across Edek's face. If Tomek hadn't been standing between us, I was pretty sure Edek would have had his hands around my throat. He wanted to argue; I could feel it. I was carrying a pass signed by a comrade colonel of the NKVD. You couldn't trust anybody, not even family. Who knew what they had done to turn me?

But he didn't argue. He held my pistol out to me stiffly and properly, grip first.

"In an hour, then, sir," he said to Tomek.

Or else, his eyes said to me.

* * *

He wasn't here.

The boy wasn't here.

You could see where he had been. The leaves were matted in a little hollow. The grass was pulled up in clumpy tufts where he grabbed it while I wrapped his knee this morning. You could see the long grooves of churned-up dirt and leaves where we came down the bank last night, and you could see the fresh grooves—an hour old, according to Tomek, maybe less—where he had been dragged away again, back up the bank toward the cornfield.

"NKVD," I breathed. My heart was in my throat. Oh God, I shouldn't have left him so long. I shouldn't have left him at all.

Tomek shook his head. "Handprints," he said, pointing out the marks in the dirt. "He's crawling—pulling himself along." He got up, brushing leaves from his trousers. "He can't have gotten very far. We'll find him."

The medic, Lew, wandered ahead, obviously trying to give us some privacy. Tomek still had his pistol out, but he had his free arm around my shoulders, his hand tight on my arm, as though he were afraid of letting me go.

"So," he said softly. "Tell me."

"I think you're the one who's got the explaining to do."

"Not really. Clerical error. Somebody mixed up some names, or that was some other Tomek Kamiński. Nothing exciting."

"Then why didn't you come home?"

"I wanted to. Believe me—I wanted to. Every news bulletin, every radio broadcast, every god-awful story I heard—"

"Then why didn't you?"

He looked away. His jawline was clean and sharp. He wasn't a boy anymore.

"I was in England," he said. "France, then England. Back to France for a little while."

And I was angry out of nowhere.

"And you couldn't tell us? You couldn't write? We thought you were dead, Tomek. We had your funeral. You've got a gravestone in the churchyard. And now it's just, 'Oh, I was in England'—just like that? You're not even sorry."

"I'm sorry," he said quietly.

"Do you know what it was like—thinking they'd put you against a wall and shot you? I wanted to die. I wanted them to shoot me too."

"Please, Maja."

"Did you even think about us? About how hard it was?"

"Every day," he said. "Twelve hundred and twenty-eight of them. I was counting every one. I came back as soon as I could, I swear."

"Well, it was too late."

"I know," he said. "I know."

I brushed away stupid tears with the back of my hand. "It's just—I missed you so much."

His hand tightened on my arm. "Me too."

"I kept thinking about you. That's how I made it. That's how I got through. I kept telling myself what you would do. 'Tomek would be strong enough. Tomek could take this. Tomek could survive this.' So I told myself I could too."

"Pretty stupid considering I was dead."

"I'm being serious."

"So am I." He bent to kiss the top of my head again. "You've always been the strong one. A little spitfire."

He didn't know.

He didn't know how scared I was. He didn't know I kept going just because I was too scared to stop. He didn't know I had cried myself to sleep in the dark last night because I had finally lost the war against my own mind.

I didn't know how to tell him.

That scared me too. I used to be able to tell him anything. I used to know he would understand.

I was scared he wouldn't. I was scared he *couldn't*.

You've always been the strong one.

I was so tired of being strong. How was I supposed to tell him that?

He must have known something was wrong. His thumb rubbed a slow, gentle circle into my shoulder. "Hey."

I wanted to shove his hand away suddenly. "Mama and Papa are dead."

He let out a long breath. "I know."

"It was stupid. They said it was just for one day—the soldiers. Just to Lwów. Helping with cleanup or something stupid like that. I believed them. I *wanted* to believe them." I scrubbed furiously at my face again. "I didn't even say goodbye. I said, 'I'll be back tonight.' And Mama said she would wait supper." I couldn't explain what I meant—why it mattered so much, why it hurt so much. "I didn't even say goodbye."

His thumb traced another circle. "I should have been here."

Then why weren't you? "They'd just have taken you too. They took everybody. If you didn't have a work permit, or if they hadn't met a quota, or if somebody else didn't report for a summons—"

"I should have been here."

Crack.

A gunshot shattered the air somewhere ahead of us.

Tomek's chin snapped up. "That's not one of ours."

"How do you know?"

"Pistol. Nobody else carries one." He slid his hand from my shoulder. "Follow me. Keep close."

My steps slowed. *Oh, no. Oh, no.*

He looked back. "Hey—come on."

"Tomek—I gave him the pistol."

He paused. "What?"

"I gave him the extra pistol." My mouth was dry. "I just thought—if the NKVD came back—"

The medic Lew's voice floated back to us through the trees. "Sir, you'd better get up here."

Tomek didn't even seem to hear. He was reading my face, eyes narrowed. He had always been good at reading my face—or I had always been bad at hiding things, one or the other.

His shoulders straightened.

"German?" he asked quietly.

"He's Ukrainian. Tomek, I didn't know it'd be *you*—"

He swore under his breath and broke into a run. I followed, throat tight.

We had been following the wood along the edge of our cornfield, working slowly back toward the river. There was a little gully at the bottom of the field—a drainage ditch, really, except it was dry now. There was a body on the sandy floor—Edek's body, facedown, arms flung wide. Lew, a little way ahead, slid down the bank, knelt beside him, and rolled him carefully onto his back.

The freckled soldier, Julian, was half carrying, half dragging the Ukrainian boy back up the ditch toward us, one arm around the boy's neck, the pistol pressed to the boy's temple.

"UPA," he said to Tomek a little breathlessly. The boy was struggling bitterly under his arm, spewing slurs and curses in Ukrainian. "He shot Edek."

"Polish scum," the boy spit, "get your hands off me—let me—"

Then he caught sight of me, behind Tomek.

He stopped struggling. He gaped at me—dazed, winded, as if somebody had kicked his shattered knee.

No—as if *I* had kicked his shattered knee. That look of sheer bewilderment—that I had lied to him, that I had betrayed him—made me ache.

"Is this him?" Tomek asked me. His finger was curled over the trigger of his pistol. His voice was quiet and calm. He didn't get angry—at least, he didn't shout or swear or lash out when he was angry. He got quiet, cold, deliberate. It was infuriating when we were kids, never being able to get a rise out of him. I was the only one who ever got in trouble for losing my temper.

Right now, that calmness was absolutely terrifying.

"Yes," I whispered, "but—"

He spoke over me, not turning his eyes from the Ukrainian boy. "How is he, Lew?"

Lew sat back on his heels beside Edek's body, brushing a hand across his nose. He shook his head. "Gone. Dead before he hit the dirt."

Tomek's shoulders were very straight.

"Change of plans. We'll rendezvous here. Spread the word."

Lew took off his coat and spread it gently over Edek's face. He crossed himself. "Yes, sir."

"Leave your kit here, Lew."

Lew hesitated just for a second, looking from Tomek to the Ukrainian boy. Then he dipped his head. "Yes, sir."

Tomek glanced up at Julian over the boy's shoulder. "Did you search him?"

"No, sir. Not yet."

Tomek searched roughly with his free hand through the boy's coat pockets, his shirt pockets, the lining of his collar. He patted down the boy's trousers and dug his fingers under the bandage on his knee. The boy jerked in Julian's grip, face twisting.

"Tomek," I managed weakly.

Tomek straightened. His finger was still ready on the trigger of his pistol. His face was blank.

"UPA?" he asked.

The boy's eyes came over to me just for a second. His voice was thick. "Hasn't your little s-spy told you? Or does she lie to you t——"

Tomek backhanded him across the mouth with the butt of the pistol.

The boy flopped back against Julian, limp and blinking. Tomek wiped the pistol calmly on his trousers and holstered it under his arm.

"Hold him," he said to Julian. He crouched to open Lew's pack. He brought out a little plastic syrette and uncapped the needle.

The boy froze. Then he panicked. He tried to lunge away, kicking with his good leg, scrabbling frantically at Julian's arm. Julian shoved him to the ground and pinned him, digging a knee into his stomach.

"What's that?" My voice shook.

"Just morphine." Tomek flicked the syrette with his fingers. "Did you know he was UPA?"

I hesitated. The boy's blue, blue eyes, hateful and terrified, bored into my face. He thought he knew what I was going to say.

"He's not." My heart was stuck in a lump at the base of my throat. The words came out in a whisper. "He's not. He's *Ostarbeiter*. He was with me in the plant in Rüsselsheim." I swallowed. "We escaped together. He's from Dalszy Bród."

Tomek paused. He wasn't all that much taller than I was, but he was intimidatingly close, and he had this way of looking at you that made you wish the earth would open under your feet and swallow you up. I had to fight the impulse to take a step back.

"You've never been a liar, Maja," he said.

Not entirely accurate. I had just never lied to him before, so he wasn't used to it.

I had never needed to lie to him before. I always knew he would take my side.

Oh God—what had this war done to us?

The Ukrainian boy struggled furiously as Tomek crouched beside him. He squirmed under Julian's knee like a pinned beetle, his breath coming in short, panicked little bursts. He kept batting Tomek's hands away, so finally Julian shifted off his stomach and slid around to pin his wrists against the ground above his head. Tomek bent over him.

"No," the boy gasped, writhing, "no, no, no, don't, don't—"

Tomek clamped a hand over the boy's mouth. The pleading turned to muffled sobs.

"Keep him still," Tomek said to Julian.

"Tomek, stop," I snapped. "Just stop. Leave him alone." Oh, I was angry. "It was an accident, all right? Stop taking it out on him. It was probably Edek's own stupid fault."

Oh, that was a stupid thing to say.

Slowly, calmly, Tomek took his hand from the boy's mouth.

"Tell her," he said. "Go on—tell her. Tell her about Bliższy Bród. Tell her what happened here. Tell her what your people did."

The boy spit at him—tried to anyway. Nothing came out. He was still catching his breath.

"Then I will." Tomek sat back on his heels. "The UPA raided Bliższy Bród last summer—UPA and volunteer militia from Dalszy Bród. They killed everybody—every single person, down to the last child. No prisoners, no mercy. It took them all day. Do you know why? Because they didn't use guns. They used farm tools—axes, sickles, pitchforks, knives. They wanted it bloody. They wanted it slow. The whole point was terror. They went around and shot the wounded when the screaming started to get irritating. They missed a few. Maybe it was intentional, I don't know. We found them later—days later—dead of exposure." He looked down into the boy's white face. His fingers knotted tightly in the boy's shirt, closing to a fist. "Believe me—this isn't 'taking it out on him.' This is so I don't beat his brains out."

Tell these *people*, the Soviet lieutenant had said to the boy last night. *Tell* these *people you're not a fascist*.

The boy had known this whole time.

He had known and said nothing because he needed my help.

And I gave it to him. I was *sorry* for him.

Tomek jabbed the syrette into the boy's arm, yanked the needle out, and tossed the syrette away.

"Get some branches," he said to Julian. "We'll have to make a stretcher."

Julian let go of the boy's wrists and scrambled up. "What about Edek?"

"We'll bury him here."

"I didn't," the boy said. His voice was low and broken. The words were already starting to slur. He gulped a shivering breath. "I didn't—I didn't." Dazed and lost, he looked over to me. "M-Maria, I didn't—didn't—"

He stretched it out into three long syllables—*Ma-ree-ya*. It was supposed to be *Mar-ya*, two syllables. *Ma-ree-ya* was the Ukrainian pronunciation.

"So why don't you?" I asked Tomek, watching the boy go slowly still. There was something cold and hard in the pit of my stomach. I had my arms crossed tightly over my ribs so Tomek couldn't see the way I was shaking.

"Why don't I what?"

"Beat his brains out."

Tomek let out a long, ragged breath. He scrubbed a hand over his face. "Because I would regret it tomorrow."

I squeezed my eyes shut. "Did you bury them? Mama and Papa?"

"I buried them."

"Was it—was it—" I couldn't bring myself to finish the question. *Was it quick?* It was stupid to ask a question when you didn't really want to know the answer.

"It's done." Tomek reached out a hand and pulled me close. "It's done, all right? They're with Grandmama and Grandpapa now. It's done."

He was lying, of course. It wasn't done. He wouldn't still be fighting if he really thought it was *done*.

I rested my cheek on his chest, swallowing. "I wouldn't," I whispered.

"Wouldn't what?"

"Regret it tomorrow."

"It's not tomorrow," he said, and kissed the top of my head.

8
KOSTYA

THIS WAS HOW KYRYLO HAD BROKEN HIM—NOT with pain, just with sedatives and a needle.

Marko was the one who wanted Kostya trained as a courier. Kyrylo was the one who actually handled the training. He handled the training for every courier on Marko's circuit because he was good at the psychology of it—as good at breaking minds as he was at breaking bodies.

And he was good. He was thorough. Necessary precaution: Couriers didn't last long. Kyrylo had spent weeks making sure Kostya wouldn't be a liability, making sure Kostya could keep his mouth shut when the Gestapo or the SS took him—*when*, not *if*. Kostya had spent the first three days tied to a chair in a cold concrete room under the constant harsh glare of fluorescent lights. No food, no water, no sleep. After that, it was three days in absolute darkness, interrupted at random intervals to be dragged back into the bright-light room and have his head held down in a bucket of ice water.

After that, he'd lost track of time.

Kyrylo would come in every so often. "Ask me to stop it and I'll stop it," he would say. "All you have to do is ask."

"Go to hell," Kostya would snarl. He'd had the feeling that Kyrylo was expecting him to break, waiting for him to break, and also that Kyrylo was enjoying the whole thing. That was all the motivation he'd needed. He didn't care about the importance of the mission. He didn't care about the glory of Ukraine. He just damn well wasn't going to let Kyrylo win. He would stand anything if it meant Kyrylo didn't win.

Kyrylo had figured him out, of course. He changed tactics. The next time he came into Kostya's cell, he came with a syringe, a hypodermic needle, and an ampule of sodium amobarbital.

Kostya hadn't known how to stand that.

He *didn't know* how to stand it.

He knew what to do with pain. Whatever they did to your body, they could never breach the walls of your mind. All you had to do was pull up the bridges and seal yourself off inside.

This—this was worse than pain. This washed over him, warm and soft and comforting, and swept away the walls of his mind as if they were wet mud.

He hated it. He *hated* it—not knowing what they could get

to come out of his mouth. Not being able to stop it. Not being able to resist. All they had to do was stick a needle in him, and they'd won. He'd never felt so completely out of control—so completely helpless.

It terrified him.

All he knew to do was fight.

So he fought.

* * *

It took four of them holding him down against the dirt floor of his cell to get the needle into his arm this time.

"You idiot," the medic said to him. "You realize we're trying to *help* you?"

"Liar," Kostya growled, kicking with his good leg. "All of you," he croaked. "Liars."

It came out in Ukrainian. Everything tended to come out in Ukrainian when he had the drugs in him. The medic didn't speak Ukrainian. The only one who spoke Ukrainian was the officer. No—the girl had spoken Ukrainian. The girl, Maria— the liar who'd gotten him off his guard. Or at least she understood Ukrainian. But Kostya hadn't seen her since they'd gotten here—two days ago? Three days ago? A week? He didn't know. He'd been alone in this dirt cell the whole time except when they came to stick him with the needle and ask questions and do things to his knee. There weren't any windows, just bare dirt walls and a bare dirt floor. At first, they'd shoved a tin plate and cup in for him through a slot in the door. He hadn't touched any of it. He'd used the plate and cup to dig a hole in the floor in the corner of the room, and he buried the food there. He dumped the water in the piss pot. It was something he could control—just about the only thing he could still control.

They figured out what he was doing. One of them had come in and found him smoothing the dirt back down. All right. Two could play this game. If he wasn't going to eat it, he wasn't going to get it. What did he think about that?

There hadn't been any food or water since.

"Give him the amobarbital," the officer said to the medic. He was leaning over Kostya, his hands on Kostya's shoulders, pinning him against the dirt.

They'd figured that out too—what it did to him, amobarbital. What they could do to him just by saying the word.

"No," Kostya said. The words felt thick and lumpy, like congealed barley porridge. He couldn't get them out. "No, n-no—"

"All right," the officer said, "you know the drill. Answer the questions, and we don't have to do this. No more needles, no more drugs. It's up to you."

"Go to hell." It came out automatically—force of habit. The first few times, he'd just spit in the officer's face. But he couldn't spit anymore.

The officer let out a long breath. "Look, Kostya—"

"Go to hell. All of you." He couldn't even remember telling

them his name. How much else had he told them without realiz-ing? Did they know about the farm? Did they know about Mama and Lesya?

No—they would have brought them in here by now if they knew. They would be making him watch while they tortured them.

Unless Kyrylo had gotten to them first.

Unless they were already dead.

The medic said, "Sir, do you want me to—"

"No." It slipped out before Kostya could help it.

The officer's hands tightened on his shoulders. "Are you going to answer the questions?"

What was he supposed to do? They would kill him once he talked—once they got what they needed. Payback for Bliższy Bród. They would cut his throat and hang him from a lamppost for the whole village to see. For Mama and Lesya to see. They would pin a notice to his coat: *Rezun*, savage. *Zwierzę. This is how animals die.*

He'd heard the stories. He knew.

Except they wouldn't be bothering with his knee if they were just going to kill him. They wouldn't waste the medicine on him.

Stupid. They were just making sure he stayed alive long enough to talk.

Except the officer was always very careful about giving him the choice first. If they just wanted him to talk, they would stick him with the needle and to hell with trying to make it his choice.

"Give him the amobarbital," the officer said to the medic.

He was tired of fighting; that was what it came down to. That was what it had come down to with Kyrylo. He was just so tired.

"Wait," he said, "wait."

"Are you going to answer the questions?"

So tired, so thirsty, so hungry, so afraid of the dark.

So afraid of being alone in the dark.

"Yes." It came out rough and ragged, scraping along his throat. "Yes."

* * *

"We'll start easy, all right?" the officer said.

It was just him and Kostya now. He'd sent the medic and the other two out. He lit two cigarettes and held one out to Kostya. "Embassies," he said, "from England. Ever tried one?"

Kostya's hand trembled mutinously as he took the cigarette. The officer's eyes, sharp and cool and knowing, followed the cigarette to Kostya's mouth.

"Don't smoke it too fast," he said. "It's pretty strong stuff."

Kostya clenched his teeth to keep them from chattering. *You traitor*, his mind screamed at him, *you coward*. "Just get the hell on with it."

The officer opened a notebook across his lap and penciled something at the top of the page. Kostya tried to read it, but the page was angled away from him, and anyway he'd never been any good at reading Polish. His own fault. Lyudya had taught him his letters, the Ukrainian letters, before he was even old enough for school. They'd shut the Ukrainian school by the time he was old enough, and in the Polish school across the river you weren't supposed to use Ukrainian letters. He'd always written his lessons in Ukrainian anyway—at first innocently, honestly not knowing you weren't supposed to, then deliberately, in defiance. The exasperation in Miss Kozłowska's red face had been worth the welts on his hands from her ruler.

"So—name." The officer's pencil was poised expectantly. "I told you we'd start easy."

"You know my name."

"Full name." The officer's lips twitched. "All I've gotten out of you so far is Kostya and 'Go to hell.'"

Kostya shrugged. "Sounds about right to me."

"I've got this if you'd rather." The officer showed him the amobarbital syringe.

"Kostyantyn Vitaliyovych," Kostya muttered. *Coward, coward, coward.*

"And family name."

He hesitated—just for another second. "Lasko."

COWARD.

The pencil scratched across the page. "Date of birth?"

"1927. Spring some time." Panic tied his tongue. He didn't know—not the exact date. Mama probably did, or it would be somewhere in the baptismal records at the church. He knew his name day, his saint's feast day—May 21. He'd never really had to think about his actual birthday before. "I don't know the day. I don't know." The syringe waited, waited, waited.

The officer didn't even look up. His pencil moved steadily, infuriatingly across the page. "Place of birth?"

"Why?"

The pencil paused. "What?"

Kostya's hands were trembling again. The cigarette shook. "'Date of birth. Place of birth. Full name.' So? Why the hell do you need to know? What the hell's it got to do with anything? Just ask me the damn questions and shoot me or hang me or whatever you're going to do with me."

"This is for the Red Cross—so we can notify them you're being held as a prisoner of war. They'll be able to notify your combat group, maybe your family—"

"Leave my family the hell alone."

"Look, Kostya—"

"Just ask me the damn questions."

"All right. We'll do it your way." The officer snapped the notebook shut. "You told Maria you're with L'viv Group. Do you know why I have a hard time believing that?"

"Because I'm a dirty, lying savage?"

"Because we're ninety kilometers from L'viv. This is Wołyń. This is Volyn Group territory. And maybe because she'd already told you she was from Bliższy Bród."

"So?"

"So you needed her help. You didn't want her knowing what you'd done to her village, to her family—"

Kostya's hands clenched. "I didn't have anything to do with Bliższy Bród."

"So prove it."

"How the hell am I supposed to prove it?"

"Tell me what you're doing here. That would be a good place to start." The officer pulled on his cigarette. "Courier?"

"I deserted."

The officer glanced up. His eyes cut into Kostya the same way Marko's always did—right down to the bone, like scalpels. "You know, I've dealt with deserters before. Russians, Germans— even a couple of your people. They've all had one thing in common. Want to guess?"

Kostya looked away, trying to keep his hand steady while he took a drag. No good. His fingers trembled. His head ached with the rush of nicotine. "I'm guessing I haven't got it, whatever it is."

"I've never had to drag a story out of a deserter. They've all got this need to talk—like a compulsion. The hardest thing is getting them to shut up." The officer flicked the ash from his cigarette. "And there are a couple other problems with this picture. One—you shot my second-in-command instead of surrendering, which means you weren't planning on surrendering to *us*. I don't think you were planning on surrendering to the Reds either, if that knee's any indication, and you were running the wrong way to be surrendering to the Germans. Which leads to problem two—your original problem actually, the problem of your being *here*, ninety kilometers east of L'viv. If you were deserting, why did you come east? Why didn't you head for the mountains?"

Kostya's throat was tight—frustration and fear and fury knotted in a solid lump at the root of his tongue. "My compass must have been wrong."

"Tell me what you're doing here, Kostya," the officer said quietly.

They would kill Mama and Lesya. They would make him watch. Then they would kill him. Payback for Bliższy Bród.

The officer was reaching for the syringe.

"I was going home," Kostya said.

The officer paused.

"I was going home." Kostya's hands shook. The words came out in clumps. "He was making me give him the messages—Kyry—Lys, I mean, one of the *royovi*—one of the—" He grasped uselessly for the Polish words. "He's—he's—"

"One of the squad leaders," the officer said softly.

"Squad leader. He was making me give him the messages before I turned them in to my commander. He found out—my commander. I was sloppy. He found out. Made me spill the whole thing." Kostya swallowed. His temples throbbed. "I was going to get them out—Mama and Lesya. My sister Lesya. I was going home to get them out."

"Home is . . ."

"Dalszy Bród."

The officer pulled thoughtfully on his cigarette. "So how did you end up in L'viv Group?"

"I—I knew Lys. Before the war."

"And Lys is from L'viv."

"Yeah."

"Have a lot of friends in L'viv?"

He'd walked right into it.

"No, I just—he was—we—our families—"

"How many times did you go to L'viv before the war?"

Panic clawed up Kostya's throat. If they knew Kyrylo was his cousin—if they knew Kyrylo was his cousin and a squad leader—if they thought he, like Kyrylo, his cousin the squad leader, was a true believer . . .

But if they knew he was lying—if they thought he was trying to protect him . . .

He couldn't think. He couldn't *think*.

"I grew up here," the officer said, "in Bliższy Bród. I never saw L'viv until last year."

Kostya looked away. Stupid hot tears brimmed on his eyelids. "So I'm lying. Shoot me."

The officer's eyes bored into him. He could feel them. "Kostya, I want to believe you. But you've got to help me out a little here."

"Go to hell." He ached with the need to hurt the officer. It would be so easy—to lunge up and grab his neck and—twist, snap, just like that. To bash his teeth in. To grab his pistol and smash his stupid, knowing face to bloody pulp. *You want me to answer your questions? All right, here, I'll answer your damn questions.*

But he didn't. Of course he didn't. He scrubbed the tears away furiously with the back of his hand, brought the cigarette to his lips, and sucked another shuddering drag.

The officer leaned over and eased the cigarette very gently from Kostya's trembling fingers.

"Why aren't you eating?"

That caught him off guard. "What?"

"You heard me." The officer stubbed the cigarette out in the dirt and returned it to his breast pocket. "I've got eyes. I'm not stupid. I bet you've got a hell of a headache trying to smoke that on an empty stomach."

And Kostya exploded.

"What the hell? What the hell am I supposed to do—beg? Is that what this is about—teaching me some kind of lesson? Some kind of stupid lesson about my place? I can eat if I get on my knees and beg you for it, is that—"

The officer got up. Kostya lurched back reflexively—*coward*—but the officer ignored him. He thumped a fist on the cell door.

The door opened. The quiet, freckle-faced one was on guard duty outside. He was the one Kostya was the most afraid of. Quiet was dangerous. They were all angry about the one he'd killed—the second-in-command, which he hadn't known until just now—but the others were predictable about it. They hated him, and they showed it. The freckled one hated him and was very careful not to show it, which meant it was all just bottled up inside like a Molotov cocktail, building and building, waiting to be set off.

"Yes, sir?" Freckle Face didn't even look at Kostya.

The officer went out, shutting the door behind him. Their muffled voices drifted up and down the corridor outside. They were arguing—Kostya could tell by the way their voices went back and forth like a firefight—but they were being very careful to keep it down, which meant they were arguing about him. He couldn't hear what they said. He could have if he wanted to—if he put his ear against the door the way he and Lyudya used to do when Lesya, the eldest, was sitting up late downstairs with Yuriy Kravchuk. But he didn't. He could, but he chose not to. That was what mattered. One more thing he could control.

The officer came back in, hooking the door shut with his foot because his hands were full. He had bread and a wrinkled red apple and half a blood sausage and a canteen. He dumped them all down in front of Kostya. He was angry.

"Two sides to every story," he said. "Julian told me what you were doing." His face went cold and hard when he was angry. His voice got calm, scarily calm. "Nobody in this outfit wastes food. If you were my soldier, I'd be taking it out of your pay."

"Go to hell," Kostya said without conviction.

"You're going to eat. I'll feed you like a little kid if I have to. But you're going to eat."

"Try it," Kostya suggested.

"Just eat, Kostya," the officer said wearily.

And Kostya did.

He could tell himself it was because he knew they could just drug him and force it down his throat anyway or because now they knew his full name and where his family lived—but the truth was it was because he was hungry.

The officer watched him—smoked a cigarette and watched him, eyes cool.

"Tell me about Lys," he said. "Tell me how you met."

That was the moment Kostya realized it had been a trick, the whole thing—so the officer could come swooping in to save him, so he would be duly grateful—and also the moment he realized he didn't care.

"He's my cousin," he mumbled around a crumbly mouthful of bread. "Kyrylo Romaniuk. He's from L'viv. I mean he lives in L'viv. He wasn't born there. They sent him to the orphanage there after the terrorist attacks."

"The terrorist attacks." The officer's eyes narrowed, assessing. "'They' were the police? Polish police? You're talking about—"

"Police, army, whatever." Kostya shrugged. "The pacification. After that train got blown up—back in the thirties. When they came and burned all the farms. They burned his father's farm."

"His parents were killed?"

"No, arrested. They sent his father to the concentration camp at Bereza Kartuska. My aunt was in the Brygidki in L'viv. They sent Kyrylo to the orphanage."

"Was he involved?"

"You mean with the terrorists?"

"They were Ukrainian nationalists," the officer said. "It's interesting that you'd make that distinction."

"He was a kid. He was nine. What the hell do you think?"

"Nine is old enough. You were—what? Twelve when you joined the UPA? Thirteen?"

"He didn't have anything to do with it. He didn't join up until after the war started. He was in university. He was a student."

"Studying what?"

"Law, I guess. He's going to be a lawyer. I mean before the war he was going to be a lawyer. He's got an uncle in Canada who was paying for his—for the—" The Polish slipped away from him again. "The fee for the classes."

"Tuition."

Kostya flapped an impatient hand, scattering crumbs. "He didn't have anything to do with it."

"Because he didn't want to or because he didn't have the opportunity?"

"Why the hell does it matter? Why are we even talking about him? What the hell does he have to do with any—"

"Does he know your handwriting?" the officer asked.

Kostya blinked. "What?"

"If you wrote him. Would he recognize your handwriting?"

He would, of course. Kostya's handwriting was singularly terrible. Each character was a battle, and he lost some of them. *Durnyy selyuk*, Dima would always say, stupid peasant, and Kyrylo would make some stupid joke about having to decode Kostya's decoding. But he always made Kostya do the decoding anyway. "You can do it faster," he would say, which of course was a lie. He was just making sure he had Kostya as a scapegoat if Marko ever found out he was intercepting the messages: *Me? I'm not the one decoding them.*

"So?" Kostya snapped.

"Because you're going to write him for me. You're going to set up a meeting. Place, time, terms. You're going to tell him what happens to you and your family if he doesn't show."

"Go to hell."

"The same if you refuse to cooperate." The officer pulled on his cigarette indifferently. "You'll go before a Polish tribunal, all three of you, and you'll stand trial for treason against the Polish state. You're all Polish citizens, like it or not. I've got judicial authority in your case—direct from London. I can promise you it doesn't end well for you. Your mother and your sister might get away with prison sentences if they can prove they've never taken up arms, but you—"

"He won't come." Kostya's mouth was ashes. "He won't come. There's no point."

"You don't think he'll come for you?"

He probably would—just to carry out the execution

personally. "He knows what I did. He knows I ratted him out to the commander. He was going to kill us himself. There's no point."

"You'd better hope you can change his mind," the officer said.

9
MARIA

I THINK TOMEK WAS A LITTLE ASHAMED, AT FIRST,
to have me there in the bunker with the rest of his squad—
ashamed for my sake, I mean, not ashamed *of* me. He offered to
ask around for somebody who could give me a proper place
to stay. His word, *proper*. There was a family he knew over in
Radziwiłłów who might be able to spare a room. I didn't have to
live in a bunker in the woods.

I asked how often I would see him if I went to Radziwiłłów.
Not very often, he admitted, probably just once or twice a
month—if he took a night's leave or if a Red Cross shipment
came in. I said I would go if he wanted me to go. He gave me that
knife-blade look and asked what *I* wanted.

It hurt that he had to ask.

I wasn't sure I could explain it to him—how much I would rather be here in this bunker, this dark, dirty bunker that forever smelled of mildew and old socks and pine sap, than in Radziwiłłów with some proper Polish family in some proper Polish house, where every waking moment would remind me that *my* proper Polish house was a pile of charred chimney stones and that *my* proper Polish family was moldering in hasty graves in what had been our front yard.

So I told him what I knew he could understand, that even this bunker was heaven compared to the barracks at the Opel plant. He could understand that at least theoretically—how heavenly it was to go to sleep free of the fear of air-raid sirens and incendiary bombs. How heavenly to wake up free of the fear that some other wretched girl had tried to escape in the night and her battered body was now hanging on the compound fence as a warning to the rest of us. How heavenly it was to eat each meal free of the fear that one of the boys would come and take your food as payment if you wouldn't give him the other thing. Anybody could have understood *theoretically*.

In any case he didn't ask for further explanation, and he didn't make me go.

* * *

His door was always shut this time of night—suppertime, when everybody else who was off duty was squeezed into the common room, listening to Warsaw on the wireless. (*Common room* gives the wrong idea. It wasn't really a room in the proper sense, just the one place in the entire bunker that had been shored up all around with wood planks so as to feel marginally less hole-like.) Tomek had his own wireless set. I wasn't exactly sure what he was doing or whom he was talking to when he shut himself up behind his door away from the rest of us, but it was dreadfully important. They had all stressed this to me in hushed tones of awe. Tomek was what they called Silent Unseen—a trained special-operations agent parachuted in from England—and his orders came directly from the war ministry in London.

It gave him a sort of saintlike authority around here. Saint Tomasz of Special Operations. I still hadn't gotten used to it. I didn't think I would ever get used to it. He was just Tomek, my big brother, Tomek. I didn't want to think of him as anything else, anything more. I didn't want anybody or anything else to have a claim on him.

I needed him so badly. I didn't want to entertain the possibility that perhaps he didn't need me quite as much.

The procedure, Lew had instructed me very carefully, was to knock twice, wait for the all clear to enter, open the door, hold the plate out, and close the door again, all in one extended motion and without ever actually looking—honestly, as if you were treading holy ground. I couldn't help feeling Tomek let them go on like this just for his own wicked amusement, but

Lew looked hurt when I laughed, so for his sake I was taking it seriously.

Tomek saved me the trouble. He came up the passage just as I was about to knock—up from the direction of the storeroom where they were keeping the Ukrainian boy. He didn't look very saintlike at the moment. He was tugging at the collar of his uniform as if it were strangling him. He looked disheveled and tired. His face was drawn.

"Good timing," he said. "We need to talk."

He fumbled with his keys and opened the door for me—permission to enter the sanctum. It was anticlimactic, really, after all this mystery and tiptoeing awe. His quarters looked just like everybody else's. Dirt walls, dirt floor, smell of must and pine. There was a wooden bunk, unmade, and a scrap of mirrored glass and his shaving kit balanced carefully on an upturned crate, and a crucifix—*our* crucifix, the brass one that used to hang in the big room of our house—stuck in a little carved-out hollow in the wall above the bunk. The only real difference was he had a desk and chair. The most interesting thing was the wireless set—

Oh-*ho*, no—take that back.

The most interesting thing was the photograph taped on the mirror.

It was a color photograph of a *girl*—a pretty auburn-headed girl, smiling but very official-looking in a uniform. There was Tomek's name, spelled the English way—*Tommy*—then a long scrawl, all English, then a spidery signature at the bottom right corner: *Lilian*.

"What does it say?" I asked.

He was at the desk, unbuckling his gun belt, not looking at me. He was looking at a scrap of paper he had taken out of his breast pocket. "What?"

"I've got Lilian and Tommy. What does the rest of it say?"

Ha—the way his chin jerked up like a startled deer's. "It says, 'None of your business.'"

"Nice try. This is fascinating." I put his plate on the desk and stooped exaggeratedly for a closer look at the photo. "Is she Silent Unseen too?"

He slung the belt over his chair and started at his jacket buttons. "Silent Unseen are all Polish by definition. But she's special operations, yes."

"A spy?"

"Not a field agent if that's what you mean. She works in the London office."

I sat on the edge of his bunk, propping my elbows on the desk and batting my eyelashes at him like a schoolgirl. "So you didn't meet on a mission or anything thrilling like that."

"Depends on your definition of thrilling." His jacket followed the holster over the back of the chair.

"A dance. A dinner party. The beach at Brighton. The Grand National."

"This isn't actually what I wanted to talk—"

"The Wimbledon championships. I'm just going to name every English thing I know. Punting on the Thames."

He smiled finally, though it was a bit worn around the edges. I wondered when he slept last. "She's a translator. We met in an interrogation room when I first got to England. Half of them thought I was German. The other half thought I was Russian. This was June, July 1940. Russia was still 'the enemy.'" He dropped into the chair, scrubbing his hands over his face. "Her father used to be in the British foreign service in Warsaw. She grew up there. They brought her in because she was the only one who knew Polish."

"Not enough to spell your name right apparently." It came out a little sourly.

"That's the English spelling."

"You're not English." I didn't mean to be sour, not really, but all of a sudden I wished I hadn't asked about her. I wished I didn't know. "She probably just thinks you're interesting—exotic and interesting and a little funny, like an ostrich or something."

I was trying to make a joke, but it didn't sound like one. It sounded low and jealous and bitter. Tomek slid his hands off his face and looked up at me.

"What's the matter, Maja?" he asked quietly.

What's the matter? It was as if I had died in February 1942 and somehow come back to life in August 1944. Two and a half years of my life were just gone, and he had this whole other life now that I wasn't part of and didn't understand.

I was stuck in the past, and he had moved on. That was the matter. He had England. He had *Lilian and Tommy*.

All I had was him—and he was looking at me as if I were some sort of explosive he might accidentally set off if he handled me the wrong way. He was looking at me as if he didn't even know me anymore.

"Nothing," I said. "It was a stupid joke."

He scowled at me. He could tell I was lying.

"You'll like her," he said.

"I bet." Oh, help me—it still came out sounding sour. "What are we supposed to be talking about?" Anything to change the subject, *please, God*.

"I need to know everything you can tell me about Red security in Lwów," he said.

"You mean—"

"Roadblocks, guard posts, that kind of thing." He pushed a map toward me across the desk, rolling a pencil after it. "Anything you can remember. Most of the First Ukrainian has pulled out since you came through, but the Sixty-Fourth Rifles is still there—the NKVD division—so I'm assuming the main checkpoints and patrol routes will be the same."

Well, this wasn't what I was expecting. "I don't know if I can remember exactly."

"It's all right. I just want to see something."

"Is this a test of some kind?"

"No."

"Am I allowed to ask? Or is it all top-secret spy stuff?"

"Nothing exciting. I asked our houseguest the same thing. I want to see how the data compare."

Our houseguest was the Ukrainian boy. I pretended to concentrate on the map. "You mean you want to see if he's lying to you." Oh God—I didn't want his fate hanging on the accuracy of my memory. I just wanted to forget about him. I had done a very good job these past four days, forgetting about him. I couldn't reconcile him in my mind—the boy who had apologized so anxiously for swearing in front of me, the nationalist radical whose people had murdered my parents and left my home in ruins—and it was easiest not to try.

"He's not lying to me. I'm going to put his mother and his sister in front of a Polish tribunal if he lies to me." Tomek kneaded his temples with his fingertips. "I told him we were taking them into custody. Guarantees for his good behavior."

My stomach turned over uneasily. "You haven't told him about Dalszy Bród?"

"No."

"You've got to tell him, Tomek."

"He's not going to believe it, coming from me." Tomek's voice came up muffled between his fingers. "I could tell him anything. You know that. He knows that."

"Then show him the photographs." Julian and some of the others had spent the last few days photographing what was left of Dalszy Bród—for the Red Cross, Tomek said, and hopefully eventually for a war-crimes tribunal, to show the British and Americans what kind of allies the Soviets were.

Tomek dropped his hands, scowling. It was the closest I had seen him to frustrated. "Is that how you would have wanted to find out about Mama and Papa? Looking at some UPA photographs? 'Here's a photo of your dead mother. You're welcome.' Anyway, who says it was the NKVD? Maybe it was me. Maybe I did it. Payback for our side."

"Well, it's better than letting him think they're still alive just so he'll talk—letting him think you're going to punish them if he doesn't. It's wrong, Tomek. It's wrong." I swallowed, throat tight. Was it going to be like this from now on—desperately needing him to understand, but never having the words to explain? "It's like something a Nazi would do."

His chin came up. He looked at me sharply. It was all I could do not to wince: He could cut you into pieces with that glare.

"Four days ago you wanted me to beat his brains out," he said.

"This isn't even about him," I snapped.

He didn't snap back. Of course he didn't. It was maddening, his self-control. It made you want to shake him by the shoulders just to see if you would get a reaction.

He slid the scrap of paper over to me—the one he had taken out of his jacket pocket—and leaned back in his chair without a word, awaiting my verdict.

It was some kind of message in Ukrainian, penned blotchily in uneven capitals. I spent a few minutes puzzling it out. My

Ukrainian was pretty shaky, especially written Ukrainian with its unfamiliar Cyrillic characters, and whoever wrote this—the boy, presumably—didn't seem a whole lot more confident. The characters were tangled and wobbly. He was obviously taking dictation: The stiff, formal wording didn't match the handwriting at all. Didn't match him either—no expletives.

Kyrylo, I am writing to tell you unless you will come negotiate (badly misspelled) *our release Mama and Lesya and I will be tried for treason against the Polish state on Friday, the first of September, and I have been told because I took up arms as an enemy combatant* (badly misspelled) *it is likely my sentence will be death by firing squad . . .*

I looked up.

"You made him write out his own ransom note?"

"It needs to be his handwriting."

"Who is Kyrylo?"

Tomek seemed to notice his plate finally. He split his bread neatly in two lengthwise and coated each half with an exactly equal layer of pork drippings, all with a kind of effortless, absent-minded grace—as graceful as coating bread with cold pork fat could be.

"Kyrylo Vasylovych Romaniuk," he said, not looking up, "code name Lys. He's one of the higher-ups in the UPA regional command—de facto executive officer of L'viv Group. We've had eyes on him for a while. I've met him before, actually."

I turned this over in my head. "When?"

"Right after my jump—last year. The pilot undershot the drop

zone by a good twenty kilometers. I lost most of my gear coming down, so I was wandering around the woods in the dark with
a handgun, my radio, and ten thousand forged Reichsmarks in a
briefcase. Ran into his squad by accident. They'd been raiding an
SS officer's house outside Lwów. That was . . ." Tomek reflected.
"Uncomfortable."

"What did you do?"

"I said I was English. I said I was observing the situation on
the ground so I could report back to London." He smiled thinly.
"Lilian's photo might have saved my life. Only thing I had that
really corroborated the story. That and a couple packs of English
cigarettes."

"What did they say?"

The smile slipped away. "He asked if I thought we'd be coming
to help fight the Reds when the German war was over."

"What did you say?"

"I said I didn't make promises I couldn't keep, even with a
gun to my head."

"And what did he say?"

"He said then clearly I couldn't be English. It was a joke—I
think. I've wondered."

"Wondered what?"

"If he was telling me he could see right through me."

"He let you go, obviously."

"Yeah," Tomek said, "he let me go." He scrubbed his bread
around the plate, neatly soaking up every last bit of dripping.

"I've been trying to set up another meeting for a year. Haven't been able to work it out until now."

"Why?"

"Three problems. One, setting up a meeting without blowing the cover of any of our informants inside L'viv Group—two, actually getting him to come—and three, getting him to come on my terms."

"I mean, why are you trying to meet him?"

Tomek was silent for a moment, chewing—probably trying to decide how much he could tell me.

"Lys and his immediate superior—code name Marko, commander of L'viv Group—have a kind of unspoken rivalry for the throne." He spoke slowly, reluctantly, as though the words were being dragged up his throat one by one. "They haven't split publicly yet because they know L'viv Group would end up getting caught in the cross fire: The local squads would split along party lines, so to speak, and turn on each other. They both know that. But—"

"But neither of them would mind very much if the other one conveniently got a knife in the back."

"Right." Tomek finished his bread and started picking apart the shredded cabbage slowly and methodically. "It comes down to some differences in ideology. Put very simply, Marko is the radical, Lys is the moderate." His shoulders were stiff; he was bracing himself. He looked up finally. "Lys is the one who might be willing to listen if I offered terms for a cease-fire."

That hung on the air between us just for a second.

"You mean—"

"I mean we've got two options. We can keep fighting each other while the Reds mop up"—Tomek shrugged—"or we can find a way to work together."

"Work together with the UPA."

"Yes."

"You can't."

"We've got to."

"Tomek." My heart was closed like a fist. "Tomek—they killed Mama and Papa. You told me. You told me what they did."

His face was inscrutable as always. "I know."

"How can you even think about working together? How can you even—"

"Because it's the only way we survive. Any of us." His voice was calm. He had been rehearsing this. That was infuriating somehow—knowing he had anticipated my reaction and planned accordingly. Knowing he had anticipated having to soothe me. "You know what the Reds did to Dalszy Bród."

"I know what the UPA did to *us*—to Bliższy Bród, to our family."

"That wasn't Lys's squad. That wasn't L'viv Group. That was Volyn Group. Different leadership, different—"

"They're all the same."

"You can't say *all*," he said.

He said it gently, but it hit me like a blow. How could he? How could he use Mama's words like that? How could he throw her words into my face like that when he knew what the UPA had done to her, what they had taken from us?

I couldn't answer him. I couldn't speak.

He reached for my hand across the desk. I recoiled reflexively, snatching my hand back into my lap.

He went very still.

"This isn't about us," he said quietly. "This is about Poland."

Not for me. Couldn't he understand? All I had was *us*.

"Please, Maja," he said.

All I had was *him*. I couldn't lose him. I wouldn't lose him.

I swallowed the knot in my throat.

"What kind of terms?"

"What?"

"For the cease-fire." I was proud of how steady my voice was. "What kind of terms?"

He loosened cautiously. "Pretty drastic ones. For our part, we would need Lys to take care of Marko before we could go any further."

"'Take care of,' as in . . ."

"Yes." Tomek dismissed this with another shrug. "For his part, he would need assurances, written assurances, that my offer has approval from London—that I'm acting in official capacity as a representative of the Polish government." He hesitated. "Which is where this gets complicated. Lys will want London's assurances before he risks making a move against Marko. London will want Marko dead before they risk giving Lys any assurances. Somebody's going to have to step out in good faith, and it's probably going to have to be Lys."

"Does London know what you're trying to do?"

"As of right now, one other person in the world knows what I'm trying to do." He smiled at me—that same small, strained smile. "London will probably hang me if the UPA don't. My squad might if London doesn't."

"Tomek."

"I'm sorry. Bad joke."

"It's not a joke; that's what I'm afraid of."

"It would be a whole lot easier if that idiot hadn't shot Edek." Tomek rested his head against the chair back. "As it is—the squad wants him dead. Julian wants him dead. Julian has explained to me very rationally why I'm making a strategic mistake—expending manpower on guarding a prisoner. I can only imagine what he'll say when he knows I'm using him to negotiate a ceasefire." He exhaled heavily—half a laugh, half a sigh. "It'll be all right once it's done—once it's a fait accompli. Until then"—he shifted his head to look at me—"this stays here, between us. All right? Nobody else. Not even Lew."

I supposed I should be happy that he felt he could trust me—that he felt he could tell me things he couldn't even tell his men. I should have been happy. But this wasn't trust. This was bribery. He knew he was doing something wrong. He needed my silence.

I traced the boy's ransom note with a fingertip. I paused after *Kyrylo*. The use of the first name was a clever touch—Tomek showing off how much he knew. I doubted our houseguest had any idea what Lys's real name was.

By that same logic, though, I doubted Lys had any idea who our houseguest was.

"This whole thing is kind of far-fetched, isn't it? I mean the whole thing depends on getting Lys to come and negotiate for one prisoner—and not even an officer, just some foot soldier."

Tomek pushed himself up and set back to work on his cabbage. "Courier."

"All right—still. Some random courier."

"Not random. They're cousins. That was pure luck." He grimaced. "Wrong word. None of this is luck."

"Threatening to shoot his cousin really ought to show him you're serious about a cease-fire."

He didn't even seem to notice the sarcasm. He wound cabbage onto his fork absently. "I've got to assume Marko has spies in Lys's squad. I've got to assume any message will be intercepted. If Marko figures out I'm making overtures to Lys behind his back, he'll execute Lys and show the messages to the rest of L'viv Group as proof Lys was a traitor."

"I was just joking." It was like running smack into a brick wall, trying to argue with him. He had clearly been thinking about this for a while—thinking it through from every angle, considering every possibility. He wasn't going to change his mind. *I* wasn't going to change his mind.

It was the same when we were kids. It was the same when he told Mama and Papa at sixteen that he was leaving to join up. Once he decided he was going to do something, he did it. That was it. There wasn't any stopping him.

"You've still got to get the message to him in the first place," I said.

"Yes."

"How? If nobody else in the squad is supposed to know what you're trying to do."

He downed his last bite of cabbage and scraped the plate meticulously clean with the side of the fork. "I'm taking it myself. Which is why I need to know everything you can remember about security in Lwów."

"Tomek—"

"Julian already has his orders. I told him I'm rendezvousing with one of our circuit leaders in Lwów. It's routine."

"Let me take it," I said.

He didn't say anything.

I elaborated. "You said it yourself. I've been there. I've seen the checkpoints and patrol routes." *Seen*, as in walked right into, but he didn't need to know that. "You'd be going in blind with secondhand information. It makes more sense for me to go."

He eyed me sidelong—one quick, cutting glance. It made my heart jump into my throat.

"I don't ask my soldiers to do anything I'm not willing to do myself," he said.

"That's a nice way of saying you can't trust me."

"Trust doesn't have anything to do with it. The NKVD have you marked. You'd jeopardize the mission." He took the ransom note from me and folded it into a tiny square, sharpening each crease very precisely with his thumbnail. "Anyway, there's something I need you to do for me here while I'm gone."

"Oh?"

"I need you to help Lew keep the houseguest alive. Make sure he's eating. Maybe just talk to him every once in a while."

I froze. "What?"

"He needs somebody to talk to—somebody who knows Ukrainian. Lew's intentions are good. His Ukrainian is terrible."

"No."

"It'll help, talking to him." Tomek's voice was quiet. "Both of you. It'll help."

How was it supposed to help? I would look at him and see my murdered parents. I would look at him and see what his people had done to mine. How on earth was that supposed to *help*?

I swallowed my panic carefully. "What am I talking about?"

"About anything." Tomek paused, considering. "Not about Dalszy Bród. Not yet. Not like this."

"You want me to fraternize with the enemy?"

His brow furrowed. "He's a scared kid trying to be brave, just like the rest of us."

He had this way of making you feel you were about two centimeters tall. He always had an answer for everything. He was always right.

Sometimes, just for a second, I wished he could be wrong.

"I'll try," I allowed.

He reached across the desk, holding out his hand to me.

Slowly, I laid my hand in his. His hand was warm and strong and reassuring. He squeezed my fingers tightly, so tightly.

"You're the only one I *can* trust," he said.

I just wished he didn't have to be wrong about me. I wasn't going to talk to the houseguest, and I wouldn't ever have taken that message to Lys.

10
KOSTYA

FROM OLD HABIT, KOSTYA TRIED PRETENDING TO be asleep whenever the cell door opened.

That was something he learned to do during the training. Usually Kyrylo would just slap or kick him to get him up, but sometimes if Kostya lay very still and measured his breaths very carefully, Kyrylo would stand there silhouetted in the doorway for a moment, just looking, and then he would back carefully out and close the cell door quietly again and go away without doing anything. Just sometimes, but enough.

It worked for a while on Freckle Face. He came in sometimes to ask questions—all the questions Kostya had been expecting, all the questions the officer hadn't asked, about L'viv Group, and his missions, and his contacts, and the passwords and countersigns and codes. At first Freckle Face would just go away if he thought Kostya was asleep. Then he must have gotten impatient—though still hesitant to stoop to violence himself—because one of the others came in with him next time and kicked Kostya in the stomach to wake him up. It wasn't worth it, so after that Kostya just sat there looking at the wall, pretending not to understand Polish. Freckle Face didn't know Ukrainian.

Kostya liked to think he had won that battle.

He'd lost the battle with the medic.

The sleeping trick didn't work on the medic. He either knew Kostya was pretending or didn't care. Ignoring him didn't work the way it worked with Freckle Face, who just gave up after a while if Kostya didn't talk. The medic didn't give a damn whether he talked or not. And Kostya didn't dare try fighting him anymore. They would take it out on Mama and Lesya if he tried fighting. He tried just snarling oaths—a nonstop barrage of oaths and insults and stupid, useless threats—and then he couldn't even do that anymore because the guard outside the door had heard him once and come in to shut him up. The medic had moved between them and said it was all right, there wasn't any problem, and had shot Kostya a quick glance as if to say, *See? Look what I did for you.*

Kostya hated him for that.

All he could do now was glare at him silently, hating him.

The medic had started bringing in his own rations with Kostya's at suppertime and sitting there and eating while Kostya ate—just sitting and eating, not talking or trying to make Kostya talk. The thing that made it tolerable, besides the not talking, was that he brought cigarettes with him. They were a precious commodity, cigarettes, and if the medic was stupid enough to waste them on him, Kostya wasn't stupid enough to miss the opportunity. Maybe this was the medic's attempt to gain his trust. Who cared? He got a cigarette out of it. That was worth letting the medic pretend there was some kind of truce between them—some kind of understanding. Nothing had changed.

Except then there were two suppertimes in a row where the medic didn't show, and it was the hardest thing—on the third night, when the medic was back again—to sit there holding that stupid cigarette and not ask where he'd been.

"Radziwiłłów," the medic said. He didn't even wait for Kostya to ask. He *knew*. He was writing in his little notebook. He always wrote in his stupid little notebook after he looked at Kostya's knee—his case log, he called it. Tonight he had made Kostya stand up against the wall and try to put weight on the knee, just to see. Now he was writing and writing and writing. "I had two nights' leave."

"I don't give a shit," Kostya said.

The medic didn't say anything. He didn't look up. He kept writing.

Kostya was furious suddenly. "Why the hell are you even here? What the hell do you want—a thank-you? I don't even want your damn cigarettes."

The medic wrote and wrote and wrote, not looking up.

"I spent two months in a German prison in Lwów," he said. "I know how bad it gets—sitting there alone in the dark, waiting for that door to open. Praying it will and won't at the same time."

"So, what—this is you doing me a favor?"

The medic's pencil paused. "You want me to clear out, tell me to clear out. I'll clear out."

Kostya looked at the wall.

"Just shut up," he said.

The medic went back to writing. Kostya looked at the wall. Neither of them said another word.

The medic got up and left when he was done. He was back with cigarettes at suppertime the next night. He'd known Kostya was lying about those.

* * *

He saw the girl once.

It was when their shifts changed in the evening—when whoever had been on outside sentry duty came down the ladder into the bunker, and whoever was going to be on duty went up—which was right about when Lew, the medic, came in with the meal and the cigarettes. The girl must have been on duty. She was coming down the ladder, and the cell door was open because Lew had just come in with his hands full, and the girl looked right into the cell at Lew and Kostya. Lew had brought cards for a game of

Dureń and dropped the pack into Kostya's hands to shuffle, and the girl paused on the ladder, watching Kostya shuffle the cards, and then—just for a second, just before Lew shut the door—her eyes met Kostya's.

She was furious.

And then she looked away, pretending she hadn't seen him, and Lew shut the door.

It was just for a second, but that look had stayed with him. That look had been gnawing at him like a dull blade ever since.

You should be dead, that look said. *I wish you were dead.*

But she was the reason he was here. She could have left him in that barn, and she didn't. She could have let the Reds finish him, and she didn't.

She didn't have anybody to blame but herself.

But that look stayed with him.

Lew, who was terrible at Dureń, had won every round that night.

11
MARIA

IT INFURIATED ME—TO KNOW LEW WAS IN THERE every night, eating with him, smoking with him, playing cards with him. The cards hurt worst of all. I remembered playing Dureń before the war. We used to have a game night each week, and we rotated picking the game. Mama always picked Dureń.

Of course it was unfair to blame Lew for the cards. How was he supposed to know? It was an unwritten rule: Nobody talked about who they had been before the war. But I was furious with him for being so stupidly decent. And I was furious with myself. It should have been me in there. I had promised Tomek it would be me in there. I had lied, and Lew was the one having to make up for it. Lew was in there because I wasn't.

That wasn't strictly true, I supposed. Lew was stupidly decent. He would have been in there anyway.

More than anything, I was furious with the boy.

"You don't have to do it," I said to Lew. I was rolling bandages for him. It gave me something to do. For the most part, my life here was astonishingly boring. Eat, sleep. Shift on watch, shift on mess duty. Mostly what Tomek's squad did was monitor the railway line, the Brody-Dubno line that went through Radzi-wiłłów, reporting to headquarters in Równe on Soviet troop movements and munitions shipments. But I didn't have identity cards yet, and they wouldn't let me do much outside the bunker until I did.

Lew didn't look up from his inventory list. He didn't have to ask what I meant. He knew I was angry about the cards. I supposed as a surgeon ("in training," he corrected me modestly) he had to be an excellent observer.

"Somebody should," he said.

He said it without judgment. How could he judge? He didn't know what Tomek had asked me to do. But it still made my cheeks burn—partly with shame, partly with righteous anger for his sake. Julian had told me the story. Lew's wife, Nina, had been from the village of Góra, perhaps forty kilometers east of Bród. They had been part of a Resistance circuit in Lwów, but Nina had gone back to her parents' house in Góra when Lew was arrested by the Gestapo last year, and she had been there when the UPA attacked.

The UPA did to Góra what they did to Bród. Lew was in a Gestapo prison when it happened. He didn't find out until later, months later, and by then it was too late to recover her body.

"It shouldn't have to be you," I said. "It isn't fair."

"Fair is a pretty sad standard." He glanced up. "Look in that bag and tell me how many iodine swabs—the little brown boxes."

I rummaged obediently in his field bag. "Three little brown boxes."

"Thank you."

I watched him move slowly down the page, jotting numbers and little tick marks with his pencil. He did everything with that same patience, that same care. I couldn't imagine him angry.

I couldn't imagine *not* being angry. I felt I could drown in it.

"How can you do it?" I asked. "How can you stand it? How can you bear to *look* at him?"

"Sometimes it's hard," he allowed graciously.

"But you *do* it."

He exhaled softly.

"I wouldn't have wanted to be alone," he said. "When they told me about Nina, about what happened in Góra—I wouldn't have wanted to be alone." He shrugged. "And that's it. I don't want him to be alone when he finds out about Dalszy Bród."

"I do." The anger was tight and heavy in the pit of my stomach. "I want him to know exactly what they did to us. I want him to know exactly what it feels like."

"You weren't alone," Lew reminded me gently. "You had

Tomek. You had somebody. I had somebody. Nobody should have to be alone."

I didn't say anything. I didn't have the words to make him understand. I never had the words anymore.

Lew went back to his tick marks.

"Tell me how many field dressings," he said.

* * *

The knock made me jump.

I wasn't asleep—I hadn't slept much at all since Tomek had left on his absurd secret mission to Lwów three weeks ago— but it was late. Julian made his last rounds at ten o'clock every night, ordering lights out to conserve lamp oil, and I'd had time to get through all my prayers plus an extra one for Tomek. The bunker was silent as a tomb. Nobody was supposed to be creeping around after lights-out, which meant—

I slid off my bunk, crossed the floor in one bound, and yanked the door open.

"Tomek!"

"Quiet," Lew breathed, leaning close.

I swallowed my disappointment, embarrassed and a little cross. "Aren't you supposed to be on duty? What on earth are you doing?"

A flurry of motion in the darkness—he reached a quick, cautioning hand to my arm. He tapped the door softly with his fingertips. I stepped aside a little stiffly, and he slid quietly in, pushing the door shut behind him.

"Sorry," he murmured. "Thanks."

"What's the matter?" Lew wasn't a rule breaker. He was the furthest anybody could possibly be from a rule breaker. If *he* was here in my room after lights-out, something was very, very wrong.

The possibilities jumped out at me, each worse than the last: Somebody was sick, somebody had been shot, somebody had gone missing.

Oh God—he had found out Tomek was dead.

I started babbling nonsense, trying to cover up the panic.

"Is somebody hurt? I'll get Julian." I dropped onto the bunk, fumbling numbly in the dark for my boots.

"Don't," Lew said.

The tightness in his voice made my stomach flop. *Please, God, no.* "Lew, tell me what's wrong."

He let out a long breath. "No, it's fine. Everything's fine."

He was a worse liar than I was. He couldn't tell a convincing lie if his life depended on it. "You don't sound *fine*."

"I need to talk to you," he said.

"After curfew, without Julian knowing?" I was glad for the dark. He couldn't see my hands shaking. "What are we doing, plotting a revolution?"

He didn't say anything. I could practically feel him stiffen.

My stomach flopped again. "Come on—I'm kidding. You're scaring me."

"I don't even know how to start this."

"You could sit down."

He sat obediently on the very edge of my bunk, careful to keep a polite distance from me.

"It's Tomek, isn't it?" I was digging my fingernails into my palms until the skin broke. "And Julian told you not to tell me."

"We still haven't heard anything." He paused, considering. "But that's part of it. He told you ten days, right? Two weeks at the very latest. That's what he told Julian."

"Yes."

"Today was three weeks."

"I know," I whispered. Oh God, I knew.

"It could mean anything. It could be anything." Lew's voice was soft, patient, reassuring. It was his professional voice, his medic voice, the one he used when he sewed people up and jabbed them with needles. "It doesn't have to mean—"

"I know," I snapped.

Lew hesitated.

"Did he—tell you anything? Give you any orders? Just in case."

I had spent the past three weeks thinking about it—thinking through every single, horrible what-if—but there was something terribly real and final about putting it into words. "In case he didn't come back?"

"In case he didn't come back."

"What kind of orders?"

"About Kostya," Lew said.

It was like a slap in the face, hearing him say the boy's name—his name, his actual name—as if he were one of us and not *the enemy*.

I was furious again, all at once, senselessly, bitterly furious—at Lew for saying that name, at Tomek for this whole stupid, stupid plan. They had killed him the way they killed Mama and Papa. I knew they had killed him. I had known they would. I had tried to tell him. And all he could think to say to me was, *Talk to him, it'll help*—as if I were the one who needed help. As if I were the unreasonable one.

"I assume he talked to Julian about it," I said cuttingly.

"That's what I mean." Lew shifted a little on the edge of the bunk. "Some of the squad," he said carefully, "most of the squad—they don't think we should have taken a prisoner in the first place. Because of Edek. They think the commander made a mistake taking him alive. Maybe you've heard some of that."

"Maybe they're right."

"Maria, they're going to shoot him in the morning." His voice was low and level, but I could hear the tightness in it. "It's decided. They didn't tell you because they didn't know how you'd take it."

The fury went cold. "Who decided?"

"Everybody."

"They can't."

"Julian took a vote when you were out on watch tonight."

"They can't," I snapped. "Julian can't. He doesn't even know—"

I caught myself. I couldn't finish it. I couldn't say it aloud. Saying it aloud made it real.

"He doesn't know the commander is dead." Lew picked up very gently where I left off. "I know. But if he isn't dead, there's only one reason he'd go silent for three weeks."

Captured. I pushed my fingernails deeper into my palm.

"Anything else," Lew said, "any other scenario I can think of—he'd find a way to get a message through. He knows every Resistance cell between here and Lwów. He's got civilian contacts in every village. And he's the smartest, most resourceful person I've ever known. He'd find a way." He hesitated. "If it's the UPA, Kostya is our best chance at negotiating for him." He glanced at me quickly, sidelong. "And my guess is it's probably the UPA."

I didn't say anything. I didn't know how much he thought I knew—about where Tomek had really gone or what Tomek's plan really was—and I had no idea how much I should tell him. *Not even Lew*, Tomek had said. But what if Lew was trying to help him?

Lew didn't press me.

"Kostya's a courier," he went on. "The UPA will want him out of our hands before he talks. My point is—the rest of the squad know that too."

And they were going to shoot him anyway.

"That's mutiny." It came out in a stupid, choked little whisper. My heart had crept into my throat.

"It's not that simple," Lew said.

"It's mutiny. They're not even trying to negotiate for Tomek. You just said they're not even trying to negotiate."

"You've got to put yourself in Julian's head. Your brother left him in command. He's got to make the decision he thinks is right for the squad."

"Which is letting Tomek die?" The fury was stirring up inside me again. I was so tired of Lew putting himself in other people's heads.

"I didn't say *I* think it's the right decision," he said softly. "But chances are the commander is already dead. That's what Julian is thinking. That's what he has to think. And I don't want to give you the wrong idea. Realistically—"

"No."

"Maria." He was using that stupid medic voice again. "We've got to at least consider the possibility."

But I couldn't. I had lost everything else. I couldn't lose him. I *wouldn't*.

"Not until I've seen the body." My voice shook a little. "Not until I've buried him."

He didn't try to argue any more. He knew it was useless. He was, after all, an excellent observer.

"All right," he said simply.

"Lew, I need your help."

"All right."

"I need you to meet me up above in twenty minutes." I had dug my nails in so deeply I could feel the blood welling. "I need you to bring the houseguest."

I said *the houseguest* very deliberately. I wasn't going to say his name.

* * *

Tadeusz was on watch outside. He was happy enough to swap shifts when I told him I couldn't sleep. There was a bright, clear quarter moon out, but it was dark enough in the wood that he didn't see the musette bag under my coat. He paused just briefly on the ladder on his way down into the bunker, looking back at me, his face silhouetted and unreadable.

"We all miss the commander," he said.

I was glad he didn't wait for my reply. I could have shot him. Hypocrites and traitors, every one of them. *We all miss the commander*—as if they hadn't all just voted to stab him in the back.

Lew appeared with the Ukrainian boy a few minutes later. He was practically shouldering the boy up the ladder. The boy wasn't resisting exactly, just moving very slowly, with deliberate effort, as though he were swimming through porridge. He got a knee up on the ground, staggered to his feet, floundered on unsteady legs, and went down with a *thump*. He sat there, clutching the dirt and leaves and pine needles in trembling fists as though to make sure they were real. He gulped a deep, shivering breath. For a second, I thought he was going to cry. It had been almost a month since he had been out of that little storeroom.

Lew picked him patiently back up and steered him over.

"Take it easy on him," he said to me once we had moved out of earshot of the bunker. "That knee's still in pretty rough shape." He put a little cardboard box into my hand. "Here. Codeine tablets—twenty milligrams each. Basic painkillers. He can take up to sixty milligrams every three hours if you can get him to take it. He won't tell you he needs it. He hates it. He'll fight it."

I stood there stupidly with the box in my hand. "If *I* can get him to take . . ."

"Here—I managed to get one of these into him before I woke him up. Only way I was going to get him to come quietly. It'll wear off in a couple of hours." He gave me another box with the gravity of a priest handling the elements. "Morphine—ten-milligram ampules. This is serious stuff, all right? Only for emergencies. Never more than thirty milligrams at a time, maximum. You give him too much, you'll kill him. And you can bet he'll fight this too."

"Lew." I swallowed. "Lew, this isn't what I meant."

I had meant, of course, that he should come with me. I wouldn't have asked him to do this if I thought it meant leaving him. I thought he had understood.

"I know," he said in that stupid gentle voice.

Of course he had understood. I just hadn't understood *him*.

"You can't stay."

"I can't go. Nobody else has medic training. They need me."

"Lew—you were the only other one on duty. They'll know it was you."

"They'll give me a court martial," he said calmly, "and you and the commander can testify for me. I'll be all right."

"*If* I can find him. *If* we make it back."

"You will."

"Please, Lew."

"You will." His fingers brushed my arm in the darkness. "Goodbye, Maja."

I kissed him.

I caught his sleeve and stood up on my toes and kissed him, all in an instant, breathlessly, thoughtlessly—one quick brush of my lips against his before my brain had a chance to catch up.

He didn't react. He didn't move a muscle. He stood stock-still as if I had turned him to stone.

Oh—that was wrong.

I let go of his sleeve and dropped back onto my heels, face burning.

"I'm sorry, I—I wasn't thinking, I—"

Shame swallowed up my apology. That had been sheer instinct—sheer, desperate instinct. I had learned in the Opel plant: Nobody did anything for a favor. Nobody did anything for free.

I had to repay him; that was all I knew. He had helped me; I had to repay him. And I had nothing to give him except that kiss.

Oh God—what had I done? I hadn't meant to hurt him.

Slowly, he leaned in, lifted my chin with his fingers, and kissed my cheeks one after the other, tenderly but very properly—the traditional goodbye kiss, nothing more.

"I can't," he said softly.

I nodded furiously. I knew; that was what made it so wrong. I knew what he had lost. How could I have been so stupid?

"I'm sorry." I backed away from him, blinking tears. "I'm so sorry."

He let out a long, ragged breath.

"Me too," he said.

And he was gone, just like that, before I could say goodbye.

12
MARIA

WE HADN'T BEEN WALKING VERY LONG, MAYBE half an hour, when the boy suddenly stopped—just planted his feet and stopped, so abruptly that I nearly crashed into him.

"Lew?" he asked, looking back. He sounded confused.

My hand had gone reflexively to my Walther, tucked under my coat. There was no way he was going to get away from me—he had been dragging his bad leg this whole time as if it were made of lead, leaving a lovely clear trail all through the wood behind us—but I remembered the way Tomek and Julian had to wrestle him down when they tried getting that morphine syrette into his arm, and I remembered the way he nearly throttled me when I startled him awake that first morning in the wood below our cornfield. He was even bonier now than he had been a month ago, but I had absolutely no doubt he could still snap my neck if he was desperate enough.

He found me in the darkness.

"Where is Lew?" he demanded in Ukrainian. His voice was sharp and accusing, as though he had suddenly realized something was wrong. His shoulders were rigidly straight. "Where is Lew?"

"He's not coming," I said crossly in Polish. I didn't want to think about Lew. "Keep walking. And for heaven's sake be quiet." I doubted we were much more than a kilometer from the bunker, and sound carried farther at night.

The boy looked at me. He didn't move.

"The officer said we were going to get a trial," he said.

"What?"

"He said we would get a trial first." There was a thread of panic starting in his voice. "Where are Mama and Lesya?"

Oh, God have mercy—he thought this was his execution.

"Listen—"

"Where are they?"

He moved all at once—one sudden, fierce step toward me, like a wounded animal lashing out—and I pulled the Walther on him, backing away.

"One more step, and I swear I will shoot you right now."

He came up short, arms windmilling a little, floundered awkwardly, tried instinctively to balance himself on his bad leg, and went down with all the top-heavy momentum of a newborn colt.

Then he folded up limply over his knees, forehead nearly touching the ground, and pounded the dirt once with his fists—pain and fury and helplessness all balled up together.

I kept the Walther trained on him. My heart was thudding. That was too close. Honestly, I didn't think he could move that fast. Another step and he could have had the pistol away from me. Another step and he could have had his hands around my neck. I had to be more careful.

He opened his fists very slowly, sat back on his heels, and looked at me.

"Please," he said in Polish. His voice was low and broken. He held his hands up in surrender, palms toward me. "Please, I just want to see them first."

My breath rushed out as though I'd been kicked.

How dare he? How *dare* he—when he knew what I had come home to in Bliższy Bród? When he knew how it had happened? How dare he expect mercy from me? The sheer nerve—the sheer, shameless audacity—to look me in the face and say that when he knew.

I couldn't speak. I just gaped at him.

"Please just let me see them," he said.

I managed a whisper, just barely. "I can't."

"Please—just to tell them—"

"I *can't*," I snapped—so sharply that he flinched.

I drew a long, steadying breath.

"They're not here," I said.

"Where are they?"

Dead—that was what I should have said. *They're dead. They've been dead for a month.*

"In Równe—in custody at headquarters, awaiting trial." The lie slipped out just like that. My voice didn't even waver. Neither did my gun hand, thankfully. "I can get them released, but you've got to do exactly what I say, all right?"

The boy's shoulders stiffened. "Yes."

Oh God, I didn't know what was worse—the lie, or the threat under the lie, or the fact that I didn't even care anymore. I would tell as many lies and make as many threats as it took to find Tomek. I would do anything. I didn't care.

"You're going to take me to Kyrylo," I told him.

His chin jerked up. "What?"

"Your cousin Kyrylo. Lys. That's where you told Tomek to take your ransom note, isn't it? That's where you're going to take me."

"Why the hell—"

"Doesn't matter. You do exactly what I say, remember?" I gestured with the Walther for emphasis.

He was silent for a moment, looking at me. He was furious; I could tell by the way his raised hands were trembling. But his voice was quiet.

"He never came back, did he? Tomek?"

Oh, the way he drew the name out, the way he watched me

while he did it—as though he were deliberately twisting a knife blade in my gut.

Oh, Tomek.

I put the mouth of the pistol to his temple.

"Maybe I wasn't clear enough." I gritted it out through clenched teeth so he couldn't hear the tremor in my voice. "I will find him with or without you. But you will *sure as hell* never see your mother or your sister again without me. Got it?"

He was looking off into the trees, keeping his head very still. His jaw was knotted tight. "Yeah."

"Get up."

He pulled himself awkwardly to his feet, holding on to tree trunks for support. "He won't negotiate. I tried to tell him. Kyrylo won't negotiate."

"I'm not going to negotiate with Kyrylo." I holstered the pistol and shoved past him. "I'm going to get Tomek out."

* * *

"So is he your boyfriend?" the boy asked from somewhere in the darkness behind me. "Tomek?"

He had gotten slower as the night went on. He trailed farther and farther behind, dragging his bad leg. I had to stop every few hundred meters to wait for him to hobble back into view behind me. At this rate, it would take us a week to get to Lwów.

He had also gotten bolder and nastier. The morphine had worn off, which meant he was both clearheaded and in a very, very bad mood. He had figured out that Tomek was a sore point, especially when he drew it out like that—*To-o-o-mek*. He had spent the last couple of hours poking, prodding, experimenting, testing his boundaries, pinpointing just how hard he had to push to get a reaction.

"So were you going behind Tomek's back with the medic? Or were you going behind the medic's back with Tomek?"

I knew it was just because he was hurting. I knew it was just because he was looking for a distraction and I was the only available option. I knew.

But I really wished he hadn't seen that stupid kiss. I wished Lew had given him enough morphine that he didn't remember.

I wished he would shut up.

"Guess that's what they get for going with a liar like you," the boy said.

Ignore him, Maria. Just ignore—

"There's another word in Ukrainian," the boy said. "Another word for the kind of girl you are."

My stomach lurched, sick with anticipation. *Don't say it. Don't say it. Don't say it.*

"*Kurva*," the boy said. "That's what we call a girl like you."

I rounded on him, pulling out the Walther.

He laughed.

"Go ahead. Here, I'll make it easy." He straightened mockingly, holding his arms out like a scarecrow.

"I'm giving you a choice." My hands shook as I snapped the action. Tears smarted at the corners of my eyes. He had touched off a fuse, and I didn't care if he knew it. "You can shut up right now, or you can crawl the rest of the way to Lwów. It's not as if you'd be moving any slower." I trained the pistol on his good knee.

"I've figured out your problem." He stepped haltingly closer, still holding his arms out. "You can't risk anybody hearing a gunshot, can you? If the Reds find us, they'll kill both of us." He stepped right up to the pistol. The muzzle pushed against his stomach. "If you're going to shoot me, you'll shoot me, not just talk about it. So shoot me, *kurva*."

My hands were still shaking, but I kept my feet planted. It was just a word. Words didn't hurt. Words were nothing. Hunger—that was what hurt. Giving up your rations night after night and going to your bunk with the hunger gnawing at your insides like a living thing—that was what hurt. This stupid, stupid boy had never known hunger the way I knew hunger. He had never had to choose between hunger and shame. He could never understand. He would never have the right to judge.

I refused to let a word hurt. I refused to let him scare me, I refused to let him shame me, and I refused to let him think he had won.

"I wasn't finished." I pressed the muzzle harder against his stomach. "One more word out of you—one more noise—one more look—and I tell Równe that Mama and Lesya have just lost their last chance for an appeal. They lose it anyway if I don't make it back."

Absolute silence. I could hear my heart pounding. For a long moment, I don't think either of us dared breathe.

Then, very slowly, the boy lowered his hands and stepped back.

He didn't make another sound the rest of the night.

* * *

We had made fifteen kilometers by the time he collapsed.

It was a little past dawn. Thin, pale fingers of daylight poked down through the ceiling of golden foliage and brushed gently across the forest floor. Birds chattered in the treetops. It was a glorious Polish late-summer morning, clear and cool. This deep in the wood, you couldn't even tell there was a war on.

I picked my way back to the boy across the moss beds and fallen branches. He was facedown in a pile of old, damp leaves at the base of a towering oak, arms at his sides. He had been out before he dropped. He was lucky he landed where he did. If he had smacked face-first into a rock or an exposed root—

I didn't want to think about it.

I should have known better. I did know better. I knew to slow the pace. I knew to stop and let him rest. I knew to keep stopping at regular intervals all through the night. *Take it easy on him*, Lew said. I knew.

But I was angry, and he never made a sound, and I was beginning to realize we were both the same kind of stubborn.

I gritted my teeth and rolled him over onto his back. I had the morphine in my pack. Ten milligrams ought to get him back on his feet. *Only for emergencies*, Lew said, but this was an emergency, wasn't it? I couldn't wait. Tomek couldn't wait.

I settled cross-legged beside the boy, the pack on my lap. I fished around a little and brought out one of the little glass ampules. Nothing to it. You didn't even need to find a vein or anything. Morphine could go right into muscle.

You give him too much, you'll kill him.

I was still twisting the hypodermic needle onto the syringe, fingers sweaty and shaking, when the boy said, "Don't."

I jumped, nearly dropping the syringe. He was awake, watching me—watching the needle, neck craned. He looked as startled as I was; that must have slipped out reflexively. His eyes flew to mine just for a second. Then he dropped his head back against the leaves. He didn't say another word. He didn't look at me again.

He braced himself and waited, chin up, hands clenched in trembling fists.

Oh, help me—I couldn't do this to him.

I snatched up the pack and stumbled to my feet.

"I'm going to refill the canteen," I snapped. "I'll be back."

Once I was sure I was out of his sight, I hurled the morphine ampule as hard as I could into the trees. It was wasteful and pointless and stupid, but it made me feel better.

It took me nearly an hour to find water, and only after I dumped every single thing out of that pack did I remember I took the canteen out when I was digging around for the ampules.

13
KOSTYA

THE GIRL WAS GONE.

She wasn't gone to refill the canteen either. She'd left that here, empty—a last little joke. She'd taken the map and the compass and the weapon. *With or without you*, she'd said, and apparently she meant it.

She wasn't coming back.

How could he have been so stupid?

She'd been gone for over an hour. He'd been lying here flat on his back on the damp, dead leaves at the foot of an old oak, watching the sun crawl farther and farther into the sky. It was seven o'clock, maybe seven thirty. She'd probably already gotten a message off to Rivne.

Mama and Lesya were probably already dead.

And he couldn't move.

He tried. He ached all over, bone deep. His muscles felt like pudding. They'd come fifteen kilometers last night or close to it. But he tried. He tried to sit up first, pushing himself up on his elbows, but he couldn't hold himself up long enough to get his good knee up. Then he rolled over onto his stomach—slowly, slowly, hissing through clenched teeth—and tried lifting himself on his hands and forearms, shifting his weight very carefully onto the knee. Still no good. He couldn't push himself up—bodily *could not*. His mind was screaming at his body to move, and his body was whispering no.

Coward, his mind accused. *Weakling. Traitor*.

He gritted his teeth and shoved himself up, arms trembling.

They're dead because of you. Just like Lyudya.

His arms gave out. He flopped back down, breath whooshing out as though he'd been gut punched.

He buried his face in the leaves and cried.

He cried until he realized he wasn't alone anymore.

Hoofbeats echoed through the trees—*thud, thud, thud*.

Kostya lay still, listening. The hoofbeats came closer, then stopped. Footsteps followed—booted footsteps. They came slowly toward him, crunching in the leaves. Too heavy to be the girl's. Kostya lay very still. Somebody crouched beside him. Farmer's boots, not military boots. Strong hands slid around Kostya and pulled him over onto his back. Kostya yelped, clutching his knee.

A face loomed over him—a weather-beaten, wooden face, scowling down at him.

"It's all right. I'm a friend, all right?"

Polish—he was speaking Polish.

Kostya was sick of hearing Polish.

He pushed the hands away, trying to work up enough saliva to spit.

"Hey—enough of that." The hands hauled him up effortlessly and shoved him against the tree trunk. "I said I'm a friend, son. Let's see what you've done to your knee."

"*Ydy do bisa.*"

The hands paused.

"Well, that explains some things." The farmer held Kostya against the trunk, looking him over. He switched to Ukrainian, accented but passable. "*Ya druh*—friend, all right? I'm your friend. My name is Marek."

"Go to hell," Kostya snarled again.

"Not until I've had a look at this knee." Unfazed, Marek let go of Kostya's arms and shifted onto his knees, taking Kostya's knee between his hands. "What are you doing in that coat? Trying to get yourself shot as a spy?"

His coat—Lew's old Polish army coat. The Reds had taken his other one, the civilian one from Mrs. Kijek, when they searched him. Lew had given him this one.

"I took it," Kostya said, teeth gritted. "I took it when I killed him."

Marek didn't even look up. He was rolling up Kostya's trouser leg. "All right."

"I'll kill you."

"You're saying that now. Just wait until I do this." Marek rolled the trouser up over Kostya's knee. His callused hands cradled the knee, surprisingly gentle. "Well, it isn't pretty, is it?"

Kostya dug his fingers into the dirt, swallowing a sob. "Just leave it."

Marek put the knee down very carefully. "Is the bullet still in there?"

"Don't know." He honestly didn't. He didn't know what all they had done to him back in that cell. He didn't even really remember that first couple of days—just needles and drugs and questions all blurred together. "Just leave me the hell alo—"

Marek hauled him up by the arms all at once, dragging him away from the tree.

Kostya screamed.

"Hey—it's all right. You're all right. We're going to get you onto the mare." Marek spoke softly, soothingly, the way you talked to a spooked animal. His hands were tight under Kostya's arms, pulling and pulling. Kostya's legs trailed uselessly through the leaves. "We're going to get that knee taken care of, all right?"

"Son of a bitch." Kostya scrabbled for Marek's hands, gasping and swearing. It hurt, it hurt, it *hurt*. "Let me go—let me—"

"Just a little farther."

"*Let me go.*"

"Just a little farther. I know it hurts."

"Let him go," the girl snapped.

She was there out of nowhere. She was holding the pistol on Marek's face. She was red faced and breathless. She'd been running. She'd heard him scream.

Marek stopped, still holding Kostya by the arms.

"I'm putting him on the horse," he said calmly. "I'm a friend."

"Resistance?"

"A friend," Marek repeated.

"We don't need your help."

"Planning on leaving him here? Because he isn't walking."

The girl's hand wavered a little, but her chin came up defiantly. "We'll manage."

"He won't. I don't know which one of you is the idiot who thought he could put weight on that knee, but at this point he'll be lucky if he ever walks again. The cap's been shot to hell." Marek's voice was quiet and level. "If he wants a chance, he comes with me."

"Comes where?"

"My farm. Across the river."

"I saw the farm." Her gaze slid from Marek to the horse, then back again, calculating. "What are you doing out here?"

"I tell you my business, you tell me yours."

The girl's mouth tightened.

"Come on," Marek said. "We can talk. Both of you look like you could eat."

The girl's eyes fell on Kostya's just for a second. She seemed to make up her mind all at once. She lowered the pistol.

"All right," she said stiffly. "We'll talk."

"Help me get him on the mare," Marek said.

* * *

The farm looked so much like home—so much like what he remembered of home—that it made Kostya's throat ache: the little clay farmhouse, plain but tidy, with its four bright, clean whitewashed walls; the clapboard barn nestled right against the kitchen wall so the heat from the stove and oven would keep the hen boxes warm in wintertime; the families of sparrows nesting in the roof thatch and the stork's nest atop the ridge of the barn. It smelled like home too: woodsmoke and cut hay and manure and, in the kitchen, rye bread and dried herbs—dill and parsley and thyme in little bunches hung from the timber trusses.

If he closed his eyes it could be home. If he closed his eyes it could be five years ago, August 1939. They would all be here with him, Papa and Mama and Lesya and Lyudya, all together with him, and they would never have heard of any of it or thought about any of it—Nazis or Soviets or the UPA or death squads or labor camps or *Untermenschen* or *Ostarbeiter*. They would be thinking about the harvest, and about the winter to come, and about making the seed money last, because that was what you thought about in August in Bród, and it would be all right because it had always been all right, and they would all be together.

But of course when he opened his eyes it would be 1944 again, and Papa would be dead, and Lyudya would be dead, and it would just be him—him and this girl, this bitter, angry Polish girl trying to make him pay for her dead family by taking what was left of his, this girl who hated herself so much for saving his life that night in the barn.

He was stupid to let himself think about home.

She crouched beside him on the oak kitchen floor, the girl, hands wrapped tightly around her bowl of cold borscht. Marek was still out in the barn, putting the mare up. His wife, Agata, irritatingly kind faced and smiling, moved busily around the little kitchen, stirring up the coals in the woodstove and putting a kettle on and setting out cups for tea. She didn't know Ukrainian, and she didn't seem to think Kostya knew any Polish. She kept trying to talk to him in awful pidgin Ukrainian, pointing and waving and nodding, as if he were a little kid or a puppy.

Kostya didn't try correcting her. He would rather not talk to her anyway. He didn't know what to do with her kindness, the same way he hadn't known what to do with Lew's. "Hurt?" she asked him, pointing at the knee. He just shook his head and moved away before she could grab him and try to look at it. No, it didn't hurt. He'd only walked fifteen kilometers on a shattered kneecap. What would make her think it hurt?

"I'm your sister," the girl said softly in Kostya's ear, in Ukrainian. "We're from Płoskirów and we've lost our farm and our parents are dead, and we're going to Lwów looking for relatives, all right? They don't need to know anything else. I'll do the talking. They don't know you know Polish anyway."

Kostya pretended not to hear. Petty but satisfying.

"Do you hear me?" the girl asked.

He concentrated on his borscht, not answering.

"Answer me," the girl said.

"Am I allowed to talk if it's just to remind you I'm not allowed to talk?"

She rolled her eyes. "You can talk."

"They won't buy it."

"Why not?"

"Because your Ukrainian is shit." That was a lie. It wasn't bad, just slow and careful. Better than his Polish.

"Well, they don't know that," she said primly.

"She might not. He will." But he wished he hadn't said it. At least he wished he hadn't said it like a slap to her face. She'd come back for him. He hadn't thought she was going to come back.

Idiot. She only came back because her head had cooled and she remembered she needed him after all—because he was useful. It was only ever because he was useful. She had saved his life in that barn because he was useful, and she was dragging him along with her now because he was useful.

She was in for a hell of a nasty surprise. Kyrylo wasn't going to negotiate—not for him.

Still, she'd come back for him. She'd *run* back for him. She'd heard him scream, and she'd started running.

It was a nice thought.

Who knew? Maybe Kyrylo would let Tomek go for her. Tomek in exchange for the satisfaction of getting his hands on Kostya.

He tipped his bowl to drain the last drop. "What are you so scared of anyway? What have you got to hide? They're your people. Resistance."

"We don't know that."

"They're Resistance."

She was irritated. "What makes you so sure?"

"Saddlebags on the horse."

"What?"

Kostya set his bowl down with a *thump*. She jumped a little. He hadn't meant to thump the bowl like that.

"The saddlebags," he said. "Five saddlebags. All empty. He'd been taking supplies to somebody in the wood."

She was silent, considering this. "Maybe to one of the NKVD posts."

"No."

"Why not?"

"Because he thought I was Resistance. That's why he stopped to help. He saw the coat."

"Anybody could be wearing that coat. *You're* wearing that coat."

"Joke's on him, isn't it?"

Her teeth were clenched. "Look, the only thing you should be worrying about—"

"I got it," he said.

She looked away. Her hands were wrapped so tightly around her bowl that her knuckles were white. They were interesting hands. The fingers were long and slim, almost dainty. You could tell she was born to money. But the fingertips were as callused as Kostya's and nicked here and there with little white scars.

"I'm sorry," she said in a low voice. "About last night. We should have stopped. I'm sorry."

Kostya shrugged. "Thought that's what the morphine was for. Slip me a couple milligrams and I'm good for another fifteen kilometers."

"I said I'm sorry, all right? I was stupid. I was wrong." She shot him a fierce glance. "But you can stop acting as if you're some kind of martyred saint. You owe me an apology too."

"My mother and my sister are being held without trial until you get what you want from us." Kostya leaned his head back against the wall, shutting his eyes very deliberately—shutting her out. Petty but satisfying. "I don't owe you a damn thing."

Marek emerged from the barn while Agata was pouring the tea. He took off his boots in the kitchen doorway and came in in his stocking feet, ducking under the trusses. He took a pipe from a box on the mantel, measured makhorka tobacco carefully into the bowl, and stuck the pipe in his mouth. He brought over two cups of tea and gave one to the girl, one to Kostya.

"Linden and raspberry leaves," he said. "Haven't had real tea in four years." He sat on the bench with his back to the kitchen table, digging a matchbox from somewhere inside his coat. "All right," he said. "Let's talk."

"We can talk in Polish," the girl said, giving Kostya a warning glare. "I'll translate for my brother."

"All right. Polish." Marek's voice was cool. He took his pipe out and pointed the stem at Kostya. "Let's talk about *your brother's* knee first. He needs a doctor."

"We know," the girl said. "We're trying to get to Lwów."

"Lwów's seventy kilometers."

"We know," the girl said. "We've got family there, and we—"

"Save the story." Marek was lighting his pipe, cupping it in his hands. "You'll need a better one."

"It's not a story," the girl said stiffly.

Marek eyed her over his pipe. "You're Polish, he's Ukrainian. You're aristocracy, he's a farm boy. You're not going to fool anybody—especially not without identification."

"Who says we haven't got identification?" the girl demanded.

"You'd be going by the roads if you had identification."

That shut her up.

Marek let out a long, smoky breath. "Look, there's a doctor down in the village. You can stay here—"

"No."

Agata sat down beside Marek with her cup of tea. "A friend of ours," she put in gently, reaching a quick hand to Marek's shoulder. "He's not going to ask questions."

"No," the girl snapped. Her face went as red as the borscht. "I—I mean—we can't, thank you. We need to get to Lwów."

"I don't think you're hearing me," Marek said. "He's not walking on that knee."

"Then we'll pay you to take us," Kostya said in Polish.

They all looked at him. The girl's eyes were daggers.

"I saw the cart in the barn," Kostya said to Marek. "It's a false bed—the cart bed. I've seen them before." He'd *used* one before, carrying dispatches up to one of the forest squads—three hours flat on his back in the cramped, dark space between the bed and the chassis, the floor slats just centimeters above his nose, while the wagon jolted and groaned over rutted mud tracks. "We'll pay you to drive us. You can drop us before you get to the Reds' checkpoint at Malechów."

To Marek's credit, he didn't try denying anything. He pulled on his pipe, studying Kostya with shrewd eyes. "Pay us how? The clothes off your backs?"

"Medicine. Morphine and codeine." Kostya waved a hand at the girl's pack. "Your doctor down in the village would probably kill to get his hands on it."

The girl was very still beside him, tensed tight as a spring. Her lips were moving just perceptibly. She was either praying or swearing. Probably swearing. He didn't exactly blame her. Marek had humiliated her by knocking holes in her plan, and now he, the farm boy, the stupid peasant, was humiliating her by letting on he'd known a better one this whole time.

But she wasn't stopping him.

"Can't risk it," Marek said. "Your business is your business—fine by me. But I'm not carting you seventy kilometers without knowing who you're running from."

"Not running. Looking for somebody."

Now the girl's hand flew to his arm.

"Her brother—her actual brother." He twitched a little—wasn't expecting her to touch him.

Wasn't expecting it to make his heart lurch.

Idiot, idiot, idiot.

He clenched his teeth. "He's a Resistance officer. He'd have come this way about three weeks ago, heading for L'viv."

The girl's fingers knotted in Kostya's coat sleeve. She lifted her chin. "Code name Robak," she said almost defiantly. "Commander of Wydra Squad, Twenty-Seventh Infantry, Home Army—in Wołyń."

Marek and Agata exchanged a sharp glance.

"Tomek," Agata said. "Tomek is your brother?"

The girl's fingers clutched tighter. She let out a soft little breath. "You know him," she said. It wasn't really a question, more like a realization.

"Everybody knows him," Marek burst out, exasperated. "Why didn't you just start with—"

"He came through on the seventh," Agata said smoothly, "Monday the seventh. He spent the night with us. Marek took him into Lwów next morning."

"Said he'd be back through in a week or so," Marek said.

"Was he?"

Marek hesitated. "That's the last we've seen him."

The girl's fingers were digging into Kostya's arm so hard that his hand was going numb—as if she were holding on. As if she were slipping and holding on to *him*.

"Then we'll need your cart," she said. "We can give you ninety milligrams of morphine and four hundred milligrams of codeine. And a Walther pistol."

Marek and Agata exchanged another glance. Then Marek took his pipe out, rubbed the bridge of his nose with two fingers, and sighed.

"Keep the medicine. And for God's sake keep the gun. You can pay us back by finding him."

14
KOSTYA

"SO YOU KNEW," THE GIRL ACCUSED. "YOU KNEW this whole time."

They'd wheeled the cart into the barnyard, she and Marek, and Marek had gone back inside the barn to get the mare. The girl was unhooking the tailgate chain, pulling the chain out through the loops, deliberately not looking at Kostya. She hadn't looked at him since the kitchen. She hadn't said another word until now. She was being very careful to keep the tailgate between them.

He wondered whether she had felt him shiver when she touched him.

Idiot.

"Knew what?" he muttered.

"That Tomek is my brother."

"Everybody knows."

"Oh, really? 'So is he your boyfriend?' 'So were you going behind his back with the medic?' 'Know what we call a girl like you?'"

"I knew he was your brother."

"You called me a whore."

He had. Didn't remember very much of last night, but he remembered that. Being angry and wanting to make her angry. Hurting and wanting her to hurt.

He remembered that it worked. He remembered thinking she was really going to shoot him. Couldn't remember whether he'd wanted her to.

He didn't know what to say. He gave a stupid little shrug.

She hissed a breath. "So it's not that you can't help being a boor. It's that you choose to be a boor."

"I don't know what that means."

"It's what we call people like you. A boor—a brute."

"*Rezun*," Kostya supplied. "Savage. Animal."

"That's not what I said. And anyway I said it's not that you can't help it." She yanked at the chain. "So how did you know? We don't really look alike."

They looked more alike than she thought they did, but Kostya understood. People always said he and Lyudya looked alike. People always thought they were twins. He'd thought that was stupid when they were kids. Lyudya's eyes were brown. Lyudya's hair was dark like Mama's. Kostya's hair wasn't brown or blond but something stupidly in between, and his eyes were blue, and by the time he was twelve he was already a head taller. Didn't matter. They were the twins—a single unit. Not even Lyudya and Kostya. Just the twins. He'd thought it was stupid.

"How did you know?" the girl demanded. "Did Lew tell you?"

"No." Damn it, why didn't he just say yes?

"Then how did you know?"

Your eyes. There—easy. Her eyes were amber and gold the color of harvest fields, same as Tomek's.

Not exactly the same. A little softer. A little warmer.

IDIOT.

She yanked out the last bit of chain. "Why does every single little thing have to be a battle with you?"

Kostya looked away. He didn't want to look at her stupid eyes. "Last time I checked, you were the one taking civilian hostages."

Crash. She slammed the tailgate down, irritated. "Which—if I remember correctly—means you do anything I tell you. So answer the question."

Kostya shrugged. "Tried to find my sister. Went to L'viv and tried to find her when the Germans took her."

"Lyudya," the girl said, brushing her hands on her skirt. She remembered. "So?"

"It should have been me. I should have been the one they took." He scuffed his good foot against the cart wheel. "She always did the milking in the morning. We were keeping the cow up in the wood so they wouldn't find it, and she always did the milking. But she was sick that morning. She and Mama were both feeling sick. I went to do it. They came while I was gone. They said Lesya had 'valid employment' because she did typing for the garrison office in Radziwiłłów. But they took Lyudya. Should have been me."

The girl didn't say anything.

"Went to L'viv," Kostya said. "Somebody said they put them on the train in L'viv, so I went to L'viv." His throat tightened. He swallowed quickly. "Didn't care what I had to do. Just knew I had to. I'd have done anything." He risked a glance at her. "Same as you. You don't care what you have to do to find him. You do it. That's it."

"The difference being you gave up," she said.

That caught him off guard. "What?"

"You didn't *do anything*. You gave up. You stayed in Lwów and joined the UPA." The girl's chin came up haughtily. "That's the difference. I'm not giving up until I find Tomek."

Kostya smashed his knuckles into the side of the cart. The girl flinched.

"Hey," Marek said. He was bringing the horse over.

"It's all right," the girl said, not looking at Kostya.

Marek scowled.

"There's split wood behind the barn," he said to the girl, nodding over his shoulder. "That'll be our story. I've got a buyer in Lwów who will take it off our hands. He sells it as firewood. I'll be back to help you as soon as I've hitched up."

He stood there scowling at Kostya, running the reins through his hands, until the girl had vanished around the corner of the barn. Kostya blinked away stupid, hot tears and braced himself for the strapping. The really humiliating thing was he couldn't do anything about it—just had to stand there waiting for it, leaning his shoulder on the cart.

But Marek didn't strap him.

"I said your business is your business, and I meant it. I'm not asking any questions. But there's something I think you should know."

"I'm not going to do anything," Kostya muttered sullenly.

"Listen to me, son. I said we've got a doctor down in the village—a friend. He works with the Red Cross. When Tomek came through, he gave us paperwork to pass along to him—notifying the Red Cross he was holding a UPA prisoner."

"So?"

"So," Marek said quietly, "if there's anything you'd like us to pass along—a message, a letter—"

Kostya looked up. "To the Red Cross?"

"To the Red Cross. To your family."

The Red Cross.

His family.

"They're in Rivne. They're being held at the headquarters in Rivne." His voice wavered stupidly. He clenched his teeth. "Can they get them out? The Red Cross?"

Marek scowled again. "Who's being held?"

"My mother. My sister. Klara and Lesya Lasko."

The scowl deepened. "Held by who? Our people?"

"He said it was for treason. But they didn't have anything to do with—"

"Slow down, son." Marek held up a hand. "He—Tomek?"

"He said we would go on trial. All of us. He said it would probably be prison sentences for them." Kostya swallowed furiously. "Please—they're civilians. They didn't even know I joined up. They didn't have anything to do with it."

Marek was silent, scowling at him.

"Well," he said, "this is a pretty piece of pie." He sighed. "Look, I don't know who's been telling you what. But I can tell you Tomek gave us paperwork for one prisoner, not three."

"Because he damn well didn't want the Red Cross knowing he was holding civilians, did he?"

Marek's voice was gentle. "Son, I've known Tomek for a good long while now. He doesn't fight that kind of war."

"Tell my mother and my sister."

"We'll make inquiries," Marek said. "We'll get this figured out." He clapped a heavy hand on Kostya's shoulder. "It's going to be all right, son."

Tears brimmed on Kostya's eyelashes again. He brushed them away fiercely. He nodded, throat tight.

"Here." Marek handed him the mare's reins. "Make yourself useful. Pójdźka's patient as a saint. She won't mind you leaning on her."

* * *

The girl must not have realized what exactly she'd gotten herself into until the moment Marek closed the tailgate and they were shut in the dark below the cart bed, wedged too tightly to move. She lay stiff as a board beside Kostya, her shoulder braced against his.

"So you've done this before?" she asked. Marek was circling the cart one last time, checking the ties on the canvas tarpaulin they'd put over the wood, making little adjustments to the harness leathers. She was trying to sound casual, but her muscles were clenched so hard that Kostya could feel her shivering a little. "Used one of these, I mean?"

So she was still talking to him. He had sort of hoped she wasn't. He didn't want to talk to her.

You gave up. That's the difference between us.

"Couple of times," he said. For some reason, this had never bothered him—the closeness and the pitch dark. Maybe it was the familiar, reassuring smells of horse and earth and axle grease. There were worse things than lying still and quiet in this warm, dry space for a couple of hours, God knew. Best thing to do was to take the opportunity to sleep. He was doing that now—eyes shut, mind drifting.

He was doing it very deliberately because the alternative was lying here thinking about how close she was.

"What if they make him open the tailgate?" the girl asked.

"We'll be out before the checkpoint."

"I mean if they stop him on the road," the girl said.

Marek thumped a hand on the side of the cart. "No noise. Better start practicing now."

The girl drew a ragged breath and let it out very slowly. The cart shuddered and groaned as Marek swung into the driver's seat.

"I can't," the girl said suddenly.

Kostya opened his eyes. "What?"

"I can't. I can't." She shifted beside him, groping for the tail-gate. "Tell him to open it."

The cart lurched forward.

The girl panicked. She twisted, legs thrashing. Her knee jabbed into Kostya's. He pushed as far away from her as he could, biting back a scream. "What the hell? Stop. *Stop*."

"Open it." Her voice was rough, somewhere between a growl and a sob. She scrabbled blindly for the tailgate. "Open it."

He caught her hand. "Can't open it from the inside."

"*Open it.*"

"Hey." He tried to sound like Lew, calm and patient. He bent his head to speak right into her ear. "Breathe. Count the breaths. Gives you something else to think about."

"I *can't* breathe."

"Should be pretty easy to count, then."

She laughed unexpectedly—a gulping, choked little laugh.

She lay still. For a moment, there was just the groan of the cart wheels and the jingle of the harness and the dull *thud, thud, thud,* of the mare's hooves.

"I hate it," the girl said, teeth gritted. "I hate it."

"Yeah."

"Is this what it's like for you?"

"What?"

She hesitated. "When they—you know. When they give you morphine or something."

Kostya shut his eyes.

"Yeah," he said.

"So I guess this is payback."

"Payback means you deserve it. Nobody deserves it."

Silence. The cart creaked and jolted. He wished he hadn't said that. He wished he hadn't said anything. She made him say stupid things and do stupid things, and then she turned them into weapons to use against him. *You gave up—that's the difference. I'm not giving up. That's the difference between us.*

You gave up.

You gave up.

Lyudya's dead because of you.

"Kostya—" the girl said.

He opened his eyes. She'd said his name.

She'd never said his name before. He was just *you*. He was just *boor*.

Idiot. She just wanted him to let go of her damn hand.

He yanked his hand away as though she'd burned him.

"Sorry," he muttered. *Idiot, idiot, idiot.*

She gave a sharp, shuddering little convulsion. "Don't stop."

"I said I'm sorry. What the hell do you want me to—"

She threw out a frantic hand, catching at his coat, knotting her fingers in the fabric and clutching tight, the way she had done in the kitchen—as if she were holding on to him to keep from falling.

"Don't let go," she gasped. "I meant don't let go."

Her face was turned toward him—maybe ten centimeters from his. He couldn't *see* her in the darkness, but he could feel the shivering gust of breath as she exhaled. Her grip loosened a little.

"It helps," she said a little more steadily. "Don't let go. Please."

There—he could make a weapon of his own with that *please* if he wanted to.

He didn't want to.

He found her hand in the darkness and closed his fingers around hers—not tightly, just solidly, resting his thumb across her knuckles.

"Like that?" It came out in a hoarse whisper. His throat was tight.

"Like that," she said. "Thank you."

She seemed to have forgotten whatever she'd been going to say

at first—whatever she'd started to say when she said his name.
He didn't ask. He didn't care. He didn't want to know.

He wanted to hold her hand.

She wanted him to hold her hand.

So he did.

15
MARIA

THEY HAD PUT US ON THE TRAIN IN LWÓW, ONCE we went through the transit camp and they decided where in Germany to send us. It was trucks before that because the Resistance had managed to blow a railway bridge outside Olesko—ninety kilometers on the frozen mud roads from Bród to Lwów in the back of a cargo truck, crammed in the airless dark with forty other girls. There was another truck for the boys. They kept the canvas flaps shut the whole way except for once in Krasne when they let us out in pairs, under guard, to relieve ourselves while they refueled. One pair of girls had tried to run when it was their turn to get out. The guards shot them—just shot them right there in the middle of the road with all of us watching. Everybody else who got out after that had to walk past their bodies.

They left them lying there when we started again.

I think I had already known, deep down, that we weren't really going to Lwów to help shift rubble from the streets the way the soldiers said, but that was the moment I knew I was never going home.

I could still see them lying there in muddy snow when I shut my eyes. I could still hear the gunfire.

I hated the dark so much.

* * *

We stopped at some point to rest and water the mare. We had come to the road a while ago—the main east-west road from Radziwiłłów to Lwów. There was no traffic, nobody else to be seen, just kilometers and kilometers of stubbled, scrubby yellow fields and little copses under a flat, lead-gray sky, so Marek let the tailgate down for a bit. The boy shoved my hand away before Marek could see.

I was dreading this part—facing him in the light, open and vulnerable now, all my defenses stripped away. I was dreading having to explain. I could already see the stupid smirk. I could already hear the sarcasm—*What are you, afraid of the dark?*

But he didn't say anything. He didn't ask questions. He didn't look at me. He looked at his side of the cart and pretended I wasn't there. Maybe that was one of his defenses.

He took my hand when we started again, though—reached

over without a word, searched down my arm, and slid his callused fingers around mine, brushing his thumb tentatively across my knuckles.

And out of the darkness, gruffly—"Is it all right?"

Not *are you all right*—he couldn't quite bring himself to go that far, perhaps. But close enough. An earnest attempt.

"It's all right," I said.

He slept somehow. I could tell because he woke up every now and then with a little jerk, disoriented, fingers clenching reflexively. I couldn't sleep. I pressed my face into his shoulder—oddly comforting—and tried to count my breaths the way he said. I never got very far past ten without losing count and having to start again. I didn't have the patience for it.

It was more distracting than I wanted to admit, being this close to him.

No—*distracting* was the wrong word. Unsettling? Confusing?—being this close and wanting to be this close. It was confusing to touch him, to be touched by him, and to feel comfort rather than shame. I didn't think I could ever stand being this close to a boy again, besides Tomek and perhaps Lew. And for it to be this boy, *this* boy, the one I shouldn't have been able to stand—it was confusing.

We stopped a few more times. There must have been traffic on the road; Marek didn't open the tailgate anymore. We stopped once for a Soviet patrol. They spent a couple of minutes looking at Marek's papers and asking him questions. It was an awful, awful feeling—just lying here listening and waiting, thinking about what would happen if they found us, not being able to *do* anything.

But nothing happened. They didn't even look under the tarpaulin. They gave Marek his papers back and told him to be careful: It looked as though it might rain tonight. If it rained, the roads would flood.

Marek left us in the beech wood outside Malechów on the northeastern outskirts of Lwów, just before the checkpoint. It was nearly dark, a little after eight o'clock. The idea was that we had all night to get around the checkpoint and into the city proper. Marek wasn't happy about it. We had argued about this back at the farm. Marek wanted to risk the checkpoint and drive us all the way in. He had done it before. He could take us to some friends of his in the city, Resistance friends. It was harder than I anticipated, putting him off. He was sharp. He didn't ask questions, true to his word, but he could put things together. He didn't buy my excuse—that if we were caught it would be easier to explain being in the wood than sneaking through a checkpoint in a false cart bed. He hadn't actually said so, but I knew he thought I was the one who had put that bullet in the boy's knee, and I was pretty sure he thought I was keeping the boy from a doctor deliberately as a means of coercion.

He was wrong, thank goodness. But he wasn't very far wrong.

We couldn't go to the Resistance. Julian had probably put out an alert for me—for desertion if not for treason outright. I could have throttled the boy for telling Marek and Agata who we were back at the farm. We were lucky they didn't already know to be looking for us.

It wasn't just Julian and his alert either. If the boy figured out the Resistance was looking for us, I would bet anything it wouldn't take him much longer to figure out I had been lying to him about his mother and his sister in custody in Równe.

Either way, I was sunk.

Marek didn't linger—he wanted to be through the checkpoint before the curfew at nightfall—but he took the boy aside for a minute while I fished around under the cart bed for my musette bag. I couldn't hear what they were saying, and I obviously wasn't meant to, which made me uneasy.

I tried not to think about it. I dragged the musette bag out of the bed, huffing a little. "Just a few things," Agata had said, then proceeded to empty the entire contents of her pantry into the bag—bread, apples, hard cheese, jam and honey, sausage, salt pork. I stood there stupidly and let her do it. I didn't have the words to protest. I hated that it caught me off guard—people helping because they wanted to, not because they had to or because they were expecting something in return. I hated that I always assumed there was some hidden motive, some angle. I hated that my first instinct was to ask why—why would somebody do that? Why would she? Why would Marek? Why would Lew?

It was different with the boy. I knew where I stood with

him. He knew where he stood with me. Our relationship was simple—purely utilitarian. He did this, therefore I did that; he did that, therefore I did this. Kindness—genuine, unthinking, selfless kindness—just left me suspicious.

I hated everything about this war, everything this war had done to me, but especially that.

"So what was that about?" I asked the boy, shouldering the bag. The cart trundled away down the road toward Malechów in the twilight. We were alone on the roadside, and my throat was tight, and my heart was sick.

The boy didn't look at me.

"Nothing," he said.

I could have made him tell me. I could have made him do anything I said. We both knew it.

But I didn't. I wanted to trust him. In that moment, I needed so badly to trust him.

"Here—you can lean on my shoulder if you need to," I told him.

And he did.

∗ ∗ ∗

"There's something I've got to tell you," the boy said suddenly out of the darkness.

I started a little; I thought he was asleep. He had been lying silent as a corpse on the floor since I dumped him there rather unceremoniously. His idea, this burned-out old shell of a warehouse in Zamarstynów, one of Lwów's northern neighborhoods. He said he had used it as a hideout before. Nobody would find us here. The Germans had turned Zamarstynów into a ghetto for the city's Jews after the invasion. It was empty now, the inhabitants dead or gone to the camps. Nobody came to Zamarstynów if they didn't have to.

I honestly didn't know whether he was telling the truth or had just made it up so we would stop, but Zamarstynów *was* empty, the buildings gutted, the streets hauntingly quiet, and this warehouse was better shelter than a railway bridge, which had been my idea. Drier, anyway. It had been raining off and on all night. It had been pouring since we reached the city.

It was a little before dawn now. The streetlamps were still lit, but I could hear swallows singing cheerfully somewhere up in the rafters.

I picked carelessly at a thumbnail and looked out at the empty street, pretending he hadn't caught me off guard. "Talk."

"You want me to take you to Kyrylo, I'll take you to Kyrylo." His voice was slow and careful. I could almost feel him fumbling around in the dark for the words. "But if you think you've got some kind of bargaining piece—if you think he's going to swap for me or make some kind of deal for me—"

"I'm not trying to get him to swap for you. He's not going to know I've got anything to do with Tomek or the Resistance." I sounded more assured than I felt. I didn't really have much of a plan. Bluff my way in as best I could, shoot my way out if necessary—that was about as far as I had gotten. "You're going to tell him I'm with you."

"I can't. I've been trying to tell you this whole damn time— both of you. I *can't*." He shoved himself up all at once. "I ratted him out. He was making me give him the messages. Top-secret stuff—stuff only my commander was supposed to see. He was making me decode everything for him before I turned it in. And I ratted him out."

My heart lurched. "He's dead?"

"No—he knew to go to ground. That's what I'm saying. He knew what I did." The boy swallowed. "Do you know why I was trying to go home? I was trying to get my mother and my sister out before he killed them. He said he would. He said if I ever double-crossed him, they would pay for it right along with me."

"Then maybe you shouldn't have double-crossed him."

It was a cruel thing to say—callous and flippant and hurtful. I wished I hadn't said it. I wished it weren't so reflexive, hurting him.

"I was stupid, all right? I was stupid. My commander said he would protect them if I talked. I was stupid enough to believe him." He made a helpless little gesture with his hands. "He let me talk. Got everything he needed out of me. Then he put a gun against my head and said I shouldn't have waited so long to come to him. Obviously I'd been in on it, or I wouldn't have waited so long."

"Even when you told him what Kyrylo said? About what he would do to your family?"

"A patriot would sacrifice them for the cause." The muscles in his throat worked furiously. "I couldn't. I lost Lyudya. I couldn't lose them. I can't lose them. I can't."

You already have. That was what I should have said.

You won't. That was what I wanted to say. *You won't, I promise.*

Mostly—all at once but fiercely—I wanted to reach for his hand the way he had reached for mine under the cart bed. I wanted to slip my fingers around his fingers and brush my thumb very gently over his knuckles, offering him the same comfort he had offered me.

But I wasn't that stupid.

I picked at my thumbnail and said, "This is Marko you're talking about—your commander."

He closed his eyes as if trying to clear his head. "Yeah."

"Tomek said he was a radical." Then again, he had also said Kyrylo was the moderate. I had the sneaking suspicion Tomek didn't really understand the sort of people he was trying to deal with.

"He's a dog prick." The boy opened his eyes and shot me a sidelong glance. His mouth twitched. "Sorry."

I smoothed my skirt primly. "How did you get away?"

"One of the squad leaders got me out. Solovey. He told Marko he was going to take me out of the city to shoot me. Make it easier to get rid of the body."

"A friend of yours?"

"I don't have friends. Marko has enemies."

"That doesn't make any sense."

"All the squad leaders hate Marko. They just can't do anything about it."

"But why not just let Marko shoot you? Why help you?"

The boy didn't say anything.

"You were putting him at risk too," I pointed out. "You were putting every squad leader in L'viv Group at risk, ratting on Kyrylo. Marko's probably been purging the ranks since then. It doesn't make any sense for this Solovey to have helped you unless he had some other—"

"He was sorry for me, all right? For some reason that night he decided he was sorry for me." The boy's jaw knotted up. "He said he knew what it was like to lose somebody. Said he knew what it was like lying awake wishing it was you, not them. Said he didn't have to explain to me. I damn well wasn't going to argue." He swallowed. "Look—what I'm trying to say is, he took me up to Zarudce—to a friend of his, a Polish friend. I think she was Resistance." He hesitated, feeling out the words. "I think she might be able to help you. He said they share intelligence some-times. She might be able to find out from him—or maybe . . ."

He trailed off when he glanced at my face. He could tell I didn't believe him.

"I wouldn't lie to you," he said bitterly.

I scoffed. "She shares intelligence with the UPA?"

"Just with him."

"With him, a *UPA officer*. Who do you think he shares it with?"

"It's not like that. It didn't matter. It wasn't about sides. They trusted each other."

"And you've just happened to remember all of a sudden."

He made that helpless little gesture with his hands again. "You put a gun to my head and said, 'Take me to Kyrylo or you never see your family again.' What the hell was I supposed to do?"

He had a point, which made me cross. "Where is Zarudce?"

"North. Ten, twelve kilometers." The boy looked away. "Would have been better to cut over from Podliski instead of coming all the way in to the city."

"We can't do twelve more kilometers on foot—unless you're saying you're willing to take the morphine."

A muscle fluttered in his jaw. He didn't say anything.

I relented. I did want to believe him, really. "All right. What about this squad leader—Solovey? What if you just—"

"I don't know how to find Solovey." He didn't even wait for the question. He had obviously thought this over. "Wouldn't even know where the hell to start. He's with one of the forest squads. All I know is obviously he goes through Zarudce sometimes." He was frustrated. His accent got sharper when he was frustrated. "Look—so he was sorry for me. I'm pretty damn sure he's not going to be sorry for me when he's stuck out his neck to get me out and here I am showing back up on his doorstep, asking for favors. Even if I did know how to find him."

"Then we're going to have to go to Kyrylo."

He slammed a fist into the floor.

"Did you hear anything I said? Do you need me to describe it to you? Do you need me to explain exactly what he's going to do with me when he gets his hands on me? I *can't* go to Kyrylo."

"You'll do anything I say," I snapped.

"He'll kill you too—do you understand?" His voice was low and furious. "He'll kill you, and he'll make your brother watch."

I had picked the skin around my thumbnail raw. Blood seeped along the cuticle. I tore at a sliver of loose skin viciously. "Not if I get him to trust me."

"Kyrylo doesn't trust. There's nothing you can possibly do, nothing you can possibly say—"

"I can give you to him," I said.

Our relationship was simple—purely utilitarian. Stupid of him to forget. Stupid of him to let his guard down. Stupid of him not to see this coming.

He knew it too. He didn't say anything. He just looked at me. He had beautiful eyes. Somehow I forgot. They startled me every time—those blue, blue eyes. Blue like cornflowers. Everybody said that about blue eyes, I knew, but in his case it was literally true.

"You would do the same thing," I told him very softly. My heart was clenched tight. "If our places were switched—if it were Lyudya. You would do the same thing."

I didn't know what I wanted him to say—that he understood?

That he forgave me? There was a part of me that wanted him to tell me no. There was a part of me that wanted him to tell me how very wrong I was. There was a part of me that wanted him to fight.

But he didn't. I knew he wouldn't. I wouldn't have, if our places were switched.

16

MARIA

THE FLAT WAS AT ŚWIĘTY ANTONIEGO STREET, number five, just across from the Roman Catholic church. The name on the buzzer panel was BARANETS, written in Latin letters. This wasn't Kyrylo's headquarters, just his safe house here in the city; Marko didn't know where it was. Stupidly, I was expecting something secret and dark and sinister, but it was so ordinary, all of it—the tree-lined street sloping gently down to the hospital grounds below us, the scrubbed-clean sandstone row houses, the thrushes singing in the churchyard. It was so ordinary it hurt.

The street was empty because of the rain. It was just me and the boy. He sat down on the step while I went up to press the buzzer. He stretched his bad leg out and tipped his head back against the wall, closing his eyes. He seemed dazed more than anything—dazed, lost. It would be so much easier if he were angry.

"Why Baranets?" I asked.

He shifted his head and blinked blearily as if he had just remembered I was there. "What?"

"Why Baranets? Just a code name?"

He closed his eyes again. "No, that's Dima."

"Who's Dima?"

"What?"

There was no point. I pushed the button again. The *buzz* was loud in the silence. No answer. I stepped back to look up into the dark windows, squinting against the rain. I jumped a little when I realized somebody was looking back—a woman, her pale, bony face pressed against the glass. She caught my eye, hesitated, then pushed the window open. She leaned out, hands on the ledge.

"Kostya? Kostya, is that you?" She was speaking Ukrainian—speaking to the boy, not to me. She didn't even seem to notice me. "Oh, Kostya. Wait—I'll get the door." She vanished, leaving the window hanging wide open in the rain. She seemed flustered to see him. She seemed afraid.

Something was wrong.

The door unlocked with a *click*. I held it open for the boy. My stomach was fluttering. "Pretty lax security, isn't it? Shouldn't she have asked you for a password or something?"

He pulled himself up against the wall and limped slowly past me, dragging his bad leg. "She lives across the hall."

208

"What?"

"She's not with the squad. Doesn't have anything to do with it. Just lives across the hall." For the first time since the warehouse, he darted a glance at me. His mouth was tight. There was something about this—about her—that he wasn't telling me.

The woman waited for us on the landing. I knew from one glance that she was starving. It wasn't quite September, but she was bundled up in sweaters and shawls and a wool coat—layers and layers draped around fleshless limbs. Hunger made you cold like that, always cold. She looked old in the window, but she wasn't. She probably wasn't much older than Tomek. She was probably twenty-four or twenty-five. It was just that the hunger had carved lines and furrows into her face, stretching the thin skin, pushing up the bones. Her ash-blond hair hung loose and limp. She was hugging herself. She was nervous.

Why was she so nervous?

"Oh God," she said, "I thought—"

She saw the boy limping. Her hands went to her mouth.

"Are you—here, wait. The elevator's out. They've got the lights on, but the elevator's still out—can you believe it? It's been over a month." She came down the stairs, shawls fluttering. She pulled one of the boy's arms across her shoulders. Between us we got him up the stairs to her flat, and she fumbled one-handed at the door, her thin fingers shaking. "I'll put the kettle on," she said. "I've got some of the tea Kyrylo brought. And I still need to pay you for the—"

"Is he here, Inna?"

The boy's voice was neutral, remarkably steady and neutral, but he was tensed like a spring. I could feel him trembling.

The woman—girl—Inna—went very still, her hand on the doorknob. "Kyrylo?"

"Yes."

Her voice dropped to a whisper. "Oh, Kostya. Didn't you hear?"

"Hear what?" I asked sharply. I couldn't help it. "What's the matter?"

Her pale blue eyes slid over me, hollow and haunted.

"Inside," she whispered.

Kyrylo wasn't here. That much was obvious. The possibilities raced one another around my mind as I helped Inna maneuver the boy into her sitting room.

He was gone.

He was dead. Marko had killed him—tracked him down and killed him for sneaking a look at those messages.

He was dead, and the boy knew it. The boy had been working for Marko all along. This whole thing was a trick, an elaborate trick, and Tomek fell for it. *I* fell for it. We were both going to die for it.

Tomek was probably already dead. This whole thing had been pointless—all these lies and threats and sacrifices. *Lew's sacrifice.* Lew was going to die because of me.

Inna's flat was beautiful once. There were ghostly little

traces: scrolled metal curtain rods above the tall French windows, patches of elegant cream-and-gold paper on the walls, floor-to-ceiling built-in bookshelves on both sides of the fireplace—empty now, of course, but what a sight they must have been when they were full. She'd had money, she or her husband. There was a wedding band on her finger. She was starving but still wore her wedding band—hadn't pawned it. A wedding portrait sat on the mantelpiece—a smiling boy in a Polish army officer's uniform, Inna on his arm in a stunning gown with sweeping lace. The photograph was dated June 1939. Inna would have been nineteen, maybe twenty. The boy didn't look much older.

Oh God—how could the world have changed so much in five years?

Inna caught me looking. Just for a second, her whole face lit up.

"Mykhaylo," she said, smiling.

Mykhaylo and *Inna* were both Ukrainian names. It was so jarring now—after Bliższy Bród, after Góra—to think of a Ukrainian in Polish uniform. But of course five years ago it wouldn't have been jarring. It was perhaps too simple, even five years ago, to think we were all just *Polish* by virtue of being from Poland. Even I, relatively privileged and sheltered, could have told you that was too simple. Even then I knew that in some schools and universities Jewish students were made to sit on separate benches in the classrooms and lecture halls; even then I knew that in

Wołyń Province ethnic Ukrainians had been forced off their land all through the twenties and thirties to make way for ethnic Poles. But despite that, despite everything, we *were* all Polish. There were Jews in Polish uniform. There were Ukrainians in Polish uniform. It had taken this war to tear us apart in ways that seemed irreparable.

There wasn't any furniture in Inna's sitting room. I guessed it all went for fuel a while ago, like the books. We deposited the boy carefully onto the bare floorboards. "What happened?" I asked. "Where's Kyrylo?"

Inna's smile vanished just like that. Her face shuttered up cold and tight.

"I don't know," she said softly. "They've been looking for him—the NKVD. They came looking for him. Police and NKVD. They came three weeks ago. They broke into the flat in the middle of the night." She fidgeted nervously at one of her shawls. "He wasn't there, but Dima and Yuliya were. I don't know if they just panicked, or—oh, Kostya, it's awful. They killed themselves. Both of them. They shot themselves." She reached a hand to the boy's arm. She brushed her thin fingers hesitantly along his sleeve. "I'm so sorry. I thought you knew. I thought that's why you hadn't been coming anymore."

The boy said, "You need to leave, Inna."

Her hand paused. "I'm all right. It's been all right. I mean, they asked questions, but—"

"They've been asking you questions?"

"They asked everybody questions—everybody in the building. They made us all come down to the headquarters and give testimony. It wasn't just me."

"What did you tell them?"

"Nothing. I didn't know. What do you think I could have told them? I didn't know about any of it. The UPA or any of it. I didn't know."

"That's not what I'm talking about. What did you tell them about you and Kyrylo?"

She hesitated. "Nothing. I didn't. I swear."

"Inna—anybody in the building could have told them they see Kyrylo in and out of your place all the time. They're going to think you're trying to hide something." The boy's voice was tight with fury. "You need to leave. Kyrylo's a damn coward, leaving you here."

"I can't."

"You've got to."

"I can't," she whispered. "This is where Mykhaylo knows to come. This is where he knows to look for me. We promised."

"Mykhaylo's dead, Inna," the boy said.

Inna got up all at once. Her eyes were bright—too bright. She was about to cry.

"I'll just put the kettle on," she said.

She disappeared into the kitchen, shutting the door behind her. Muffled sounds filtered out—drawers opening and closing, cabinet doors banging. She opened the door again. She was pulling on gloves, a handbag on her arm, a once-fashionable brown felt cap askew on her head.

"I'm out of matches," she explained a little breathlessly.

"That's all right," I told her. "We don't need—"

"Oh, no, please—I'll run to the corner shop. They ought to have some. I won't be a minute. Please—Kostya's never brought a girl out before. We should have a proper tea." She smiled at me—a sad, guilty little smile. "Well, proper as can be. I never ask where Kyrylo gets all these things. I probably don't want to know."

I didn't have the heart to protest. It made me want to cry, all of it—that photograph on the mantel, the way she lit up when she said the boy's name, those stupid, stupid gloves. Who even bothered with gloves anymore?

"She said three weeks," I said quietly to the boy. I went over to shut the window Inna had left hanging open. I could see her below—scurrying up the street, hunched against the rain. My throat was tight. "Do you think Tomek was here?"

The boy dropped flat on his back against the floor, exhaling softly.

"No," he said. "He's either the one who tipped the NKVD off, or he got his message through, and that's the reason Kyrylo wasn't here that night—gone to meet up with him. Kyrylo's here with Inna most nights. Probably every night after I ratted him out. If he wasn't, something was up."

"Tomek wouldn't tip the NKVD off, trust me."

"Maybe not willingly. No telling what you'll do when they start hooking electrodes up to delicate places. Trust me."

I looked at him. He was looking at the ceiling, not at me.

"NKVD?" I asked him quietly.

"No, that was just Kyrylo."

"Why?"

He shrugged. "To see if I could take it."

"That's it?"

"Part of my training. Making sure I could keep my mouth shut when I got caught."

"And could you?"

"Not technically. Didn't beg him to stop, but I sure as hell screamed."

"If this was your training . . ." I swallowed. "How old were you?"

"Fourteen," he said. "Maybe fifteen by then. Can't remember."

I looked away. I didn't want to look into his face. I didn't want to look at his beautiful blue eyes.

"Let's assume Kyrylo knows not to go any place Marko will find him. Where would he go?"

"I don't know," the boy said.

"Try a little harder."

"I don't *know*. He sleeps with Inna, and she doesn't know. How the hell am I supposed to know?"

"Maybe she's lying," I suggested. "Maybe she's trying to protect him. Maybe she thinks *you're* the one who tipped off the NKVD. She didn't seem very happy to see you. She probably thinks it's suspicious—you staying away for a month and then suddenly showing back up again."

"She doesn't know," the boy snapped. "If she knew, Kyrylo would have killed her by now. He doesn't leave loose ends, and he obviously doesn't care what the hell the NKVD do to her. She doesn't know."

He was right. I wished he weren't. Everything about Inna made me ache.

"What happened to her husband?" I asked.

"Dead," the boy said to the ceiling.

"How?"

"Don't know. Nobody knows."

"What do you mean, 'nobody knows'?"

"Nobody knows. He was with General Sikorski here in L'viv. The Reds arrested all the officers after the surrender. Shipped them east. Maybe the labor camps. Maybe just shot them. Kyrylo says they shot them."

"How does he know?"

"Says he got an NKVD prisoner to tell him."

"Of course he did. He just made that up so she would sleep with him."

"If they didn't shoot him, he's dead in the camps." The boy's voice was low and flat. "Why the hell does it matter? The point is he's dead."

"You don't know that." I was angry all at once. "And I think it's awful, slapping her in the face like that—as if she's stupid for not admitting you're right. You don't even know. You don't know, so at least let her keep hoping. You're as awful as Kyrylo. You deserve each other."

I could tell the difference now—when I had truly hurt him or when I had just made him angry. That hurt him. I could tell because he didn't move. He didn't look at me. He lay very still and looked at the ceiling.

"It's been five years," he said. "No word. Nobody lasts that long in the camps. He's dead. The sooner Inna admits it, the better off she is."

"Is that what you tell yourself about Lyudya?"

"That's what *you* told me about Lyudya," he said.

He was right. I wished he weren't.

Inna's footsteps were coming back up the stairs.

"I'm going to help with the tea," I muttered.

I opened the door while she was still fumbling at the lock. Her gloved hands were shaking. The key slipped from her fingers and bounced on the floor tiles with a shrill clatter.

"Oh—I'm sorry. That was my fault." I swooped to pick it up. "Here."

She didn't take it. She didn't move. Her face was white as a sheet. Her eyelids were swollen red. Those were tears on her cheeks—tears, not rain.

"I'm sorry," she whispered.

My heart dropped to the pit of my stomach. "Inna, what's the matter?"

"I had to. They said they could tell me where he was—where my Mykhaylo was. They said this was all I had to do, and they would tell me where he was." Her voice broke. "Please—I had to. I'm sorry."

I stood there stupidly, holding her key, while the NKVD squad swarmed up the stairs behind her.

Almost as an afterthought, I went for the Walther. Didn't do any good, of course. They got it away from me before I could even get my finger around the trigger—twisted my arm behind my back, smashed my face into the wall, and wrenched it from my fingers.

I gasped; it came out involuntarily. Nothing had broken, I didn't think, but it *hurt*.

From inside the flat, the boy yelled my name.

Three syllables—*Ma-ree-ya*. Distinctively his.

Everything blurred, spun, and went dark.

17
KOSTYA

"HELLO, VALERIK," THE OFFICER SAID.

He remembered her voice—Nataliya, the girl from the bar. *Pour me one, Comrade?* He couldn't see her. They'd put him in this chair with his back to the door, his wrists cuffed on each chair arm. He wasn't going to give her the satisfaction of straining to look.

All he could see, all he was meant to see, was his file, spread open strategically on the table under his nose.

He'd been sitting here alone in Dima and Yuliya's empty dining room, looking at it, while they did who-knew-what to the girl in the little pantry off the kitchen. His own face stared back up at him sullenly from the criminal record. *Fialko, Valerik.* It was the name and photograph from his fake

Soviet military identification, the one Marko had had made for him. Who knew how they'd gotten it. Who knew how they got anything? *Enemy of the people*, the report said. There was a death warrant, already approved, and an official signature, *F. Volkov, August 3, 1944*, and the hammer and sickle stamped in bloodred ink on the top right corner. All very businesslike— signed and dated and stamped and filed. All just paperwork. That was what your life came down to in the end. That was all your life came down to.

"Pretty impressive résumé," Nataliya said, shutting the door. "You lied to me—saying that was your first time out. You've been doing this for a while, haven't you?" She settled gracefully on the edge of the table, careful not to upset any of the papers. She took off the red-banded NKVD cap, tucked a stray lock of blond hair neatly behind one ear, and opened a folder across her lap. "To be fair, I was lying too. This never gets any easier."

"Go to hell, *zradnytsya*," Kostya snarled.

She glanced up, eyes narrowed. "*I'm* the traitor?"

"You're the one giving orders, and I don't hear you telling them to let us go, so—"

"All right." She gave him a cold little smile. "If we're going to throw that word around, let's talk about the company you're keeping. Let's talk about Maria."

He'd spilled the girl's name. It had slipped out by accident when they were taking the pistol off her. They had slammed her headlong into the wall; he'd heard it from across the flat. She had gasped in pain, and he had yelled her name like an idiot. Hadn't even meant to. It just came out.

"She's nothing." He gritted it out through shut teeth. "Doesn't have anything to do with this. She's from Malechów. One of the farms. I just needed somebody to get me around the checkpoint. I told her she helped me or I killed her."

"'Subject: Kamińska, Maria. Polish national, sixteen years old, resident of Bród.'" Nataliya didn't even look up this time. "'From August 1944 known participant in anti-Soviet activity, Volyn Province, suspected in association with Kamiński, Tomasz, subject's brother.' There's a whole file. The really interesting one is this—August first. She killed five men out of a six-man NKVD squad, including the officer. You were with her. They didn't have your name, but they had a description thanks to the lone survivor. Didn't take much to put it together. How's the knee?"

"Go to hell," Kostya said.

"I know how it is. We've all got a breaking point. We've all got a point at which we say 'no farther.' We've all got a price we're not willing to pay. You just don't know what it is until you've got to pay it."

"Save the damn lecture."

"No. I need to make sure you understand. You don't get to

call names. You don't get to point fingers and say traitor. You don't get to judge. You've got no idea why somebody's done what they've done." Nataliya thumbed the page over. "That girl out there—Inna. This isn't her fault. They told her she'll never see her husband again unless she can make it worth their while."

"Will she ever see him again?"

"That isn't the point. The point is *you* don't get to blame her."

Kostya's hands clenched. "I don't blame her."

"Good. Then we're clear." Expressionlessly, Nataliya selected a paper from the folder, withdrew it, and laid it on the table in front of Kostya. This one was an arrest report.

Romaniuk, Kyrylo. Code name "Lys." August 7, 1944.

"She gave up both of them—Lys, Kamiński—though to be fair Kamiński was an accident. They got Lys that first night—in Inna's flat. He must have known something was up. He didn't even try coming in here. But he made the mistake of coming up to get Inna. Didn't occur to him she might be the one who'd turned him in."

Another paper. Another report. *Kamiński, Tomasz. Code name "Robak." August 8, 1944.*

"They got Kamiński the next night. They still had the block under surveillance. He walked right into them."

"Where is he?"

"NKVD headquarters, for now. They went to Volkov for

interrogation—both of them. Volkov has them sharing a cell, hoping they'll rat each other out. It hasn't worked. Lys goes to trial as soon as they get the local civilian court set up. It's a formality, the trial. They'll hang him. They'll hang him as a civilian just to make it as humiliating as possible. No POW treatment. Volkov wants to make an example of any captured UPA."

"I don't give a shit. What about Kamiński?"

"Volkov's sending him to Moscow."

Kostya's stomach lurched. "What?"

"He might have had a chance if it had just been Lys. Lys hasn't talked and isn't going to talk. But they've taken most of Lys's squad in sweeps over the past few weeks, and one of Lys's people identified Kamiński."

"Identified, meaning what?"

"Meaning identified him as the 'English' special agent Lys caught parachuting into L'viv last year. He isn't just some local partisan. He's Silent Unseen, trained by British intelligence and acting on London's directive. That's big game."

"Can you get him out?"

"You mean sign an order, just like that? No. I've worked too hard to get here. They're not going to find my fingerprints anywhere near this." She picked up the arrest reports and tapped them against the tabletop to straighten them. "They'll put a bullet in my head eventually, but I'm damned if it's going to be for a Pole. I might be doing dirty work, but I'm a patriot. Glory to Ukraine."

"Then do it for Lys."

"If you're stupid enough to get caught, you deal with the consequences." Her voice was cool. "Anyway, if the Reds don't kill him, I will. Commander Shukhevych's orders."

"Why?"

"Why do you think? Marko was Shukhevych's man. Shukhevych took the murder personally."

Kostya digested this. "Marko's dead?"

"You've got some catching up to do, don't you? Lys killed Marko a month ago." She returned the reports smoothly to the folder. "I'm not taking a bullet for Kamiński, and I'm not taking one for Lys either. Lys is getting what he had coming. The UPA needs me where I am, doing what I do."

Kostya's papers followed the others neatly back into the folder one by one. She was done with him. He was out of time.

"I can give you leverage," Kostya said wildly. "If you get Kamiński out, I can give you leverage."

She paused. "What kind of leverage?"

"Me. You can give me to them."

"What makes you think I'm not going to?"

Kostya floundered. He hadn't gotten that far yet.

She eyed him. Graciously, she rescued him. "You really think that's an even trade?"

"Kamiński happens to get away. Some paperwork gets

bungled, somebody leaks guard assignments to the Resistance—I don't know." Kostya shrugged, mouth dry. "What makes the Reds think you had anything to do with it? You're the one who just handed them a UPA courier who knows every cell and cache in L'viv."

"Who knew every cell and cache in L'viv a month ago," she corrected carelessly, "and who is probably thinking that what really makes him valuable is that he can tell them about the UPA rat in their officer ranks—and would therefore be unpleasantly surprised to find out Volkov already knows I'm playing this game both ways. I'm *his* rat in the UPA." She tucked the last paper away. "This isn't about what you know. It isn't really even about what Kamiński knows. He's a bargaining piece, a very valuable bargaining piece. You're not much of anything—which makes you useful in your own way. If you actually mattered, I wouldn't be doing this."

She slid off the table, taking a key from her pocket. Her head bent close to his. The stray blond lock brushed across his cheek. Her breath tickled his ear. Her voice was low and level.

"Podzamcze Station. Do you know where that is?"

Kostya swallowed. "Yes."

"Tomorrow morning. Eight thirty. I can get Volkov to put Kamiński on the eastbound train." She opened the handcuffs one after the other, not looking up. "They'll bring him alone in a staff car. He'll be in NKVD uniform. They won't want him drawing attention."

"Thought you said you weren't sticking your neck out for a Pole." His voice was hoarse. He didn't dare breathe.

She tossed the handcuffs onto the table.

"I said I'm not taking a bullet for him. If you want to, that's your business."

18
MARIA

THIS WAS THE BOY'S ROOM.

They left the little electric bulb lit for me. By accident, I imagined; it was so weak I doubted they could tell it was on when the door was open. It was a bleak, bare little room, brick and concrete. It was like a solitary cell—one step deep, two steps wide. Six steps in perimeter. There was a threadbare old quilt rolled up on the floor and a clothes wire strung in the corner, empty except for one suit jacket and a matching pair of trousers—obviously hand-me-down, worn and faded but scrupulously cared for. He had never mentioned brothers, just sisters. The suit was his father's or maybe Kyrylo's. There was nothing at all distinguishing about it, or about that quilt, but I knew they were his. This little painted icon was his—Saint Constantine, crowned and scowling. It had to be his, didn't it? Constantine was his name saint, his patron. The scowl was definitely the same. And he was here pretty regularly, the way Inna talked. He was here regularly enough for her to know when something was irregular.

Kostya's never brought a girl out before.

Did he have a girl? I had never even thought about it. He had never mentioned a girl.

I hated that I had never thought about it.

They had been questioning him for a long time.

I hoped it was just questions. I held Saint Constantine and prayed it was just questions.

Then, stricken with a sudden pang of guilt, I prayed he wasn't answering them. He could tell them so much—about Tomek, about the squad, about the bunker. About me.

Oh God, what was worse? That it was taking so long because he wasn't talking or that it was taking so long because he was?

I had been trying to listen through the door. They had him out in the dining room behind another shut door, and all I could hear was the muffled voices of the soldiers playing cards at the kitchen table and the distant patter of rain and the dull, sluggish throb of blood in my ears. The whole right side of my face was squashy and aching where they had barreled me into the wall. Dried blood cracked when I grimaced. My own fault. I supposed I was lucky they didn't just shoot me when I reached for the Walther, but *ow, ow, ow*—what I wouldn't give for that codeine now. But they took my pack when they took the gun.

The boy had yelled my name.

Kostya. *Kostya* had yelled my name.

I blacked out after I hit the wall—just for a second. They were hauling him past when I came to, and he didn't even look at me. I could almost convince myself I had just imagined it. But it had been so unmistakably his voice, so unmistakably his three syllables—*Ma-ree-ya*. And I had never heard him yell it like that before, so how could I have imagined it?

A sudden flurry of activity in the kitchen—doors opening and closing, chairs scraping, boots tramping. The card game had broken up all at once. I slid away from the door just as it was yanked open. Bright, bright light flooded in. An NKVD soldier motioned impatiently with a rifle.

"*Vstavay*," he snapped. Up.

I stepped out slowly under his watchful eye, still clutching Saint Constantine. There was no sign of Kostya. The dining room door was shut. The soldier hurried me out to the hall with the nose of his rifle, prodding me sharply when I stumbled.

"No—please. Wait." I put a hand on the doorjamb, stupidly. My head was pounding. The daylight streaming in through the window at the end of the hall was making my eyes water. "My friend. Where is he?"

"*Idí*." He gave me another little shove with the nose of the rifle. Move.

I fumbled for the Russian words, dry-mouthed with panic. "*Tovarish*. My friend. Where is he?"

"*Idí!*"

"Ma-ree-ya," Kostya said.

He was leaning against the wall, his weight off his bad leg. He limped over to take my elbow. His head bent close to mine.

"Just walk," he said. "They're letting us go."

"What?"

"Just walk."

We walked. *I* walked. He leaned on me and shuffled heavily along, his fingers clutching tight. He sucked a little breath and let it out softly between his teeth as we took each stair. He was huffing by the time we reached the street. Sweat stood out in tiny beads on his forehead.

I chewed nervously on my bottom lip. I wasn't sure how to ask what I wanted to ask. "Did they give you a hard time?" I managed finally.

"No," he said, "just questions."

"And did you—"

I couldn't bring myself to finish.

"No," he said.

Then he said, deliberately not looking at me, "Are you hurt?"

"I could kill for an aspirin."

"Yeah," he said.

And I was crying—just like that.

It was so stupid. I was crying over an aspirin. Not for Tomek. Not for Lew. Just because my head hurt so very badly and I didn't have a stupid aspirin.

"Hey." Kostya scowled at me.

"The light hurts," I told him stupidly, blinking back the tears. "It's just the light—just—"

Oh.

His fingertips were on my face.

I drew a low, sharp breath by reflex, but I didn't pull away.

His touch had been so comforting under the cart bed, so unexpectedly comforting—but that was just because of the dark. We were in daylight now. I shouldn't have needed it.

Maybe it wasn't just because of the dark.

Maybe I didn't need it. Maybe I wanted it.

In any case, I didn't want to pull away.

He turned my head carefully with his fingers, brushing away dried blood with a callused thumb. I shivered, and he yanked his hand away.

"All right," he said.

He clamped a hand on my elbow and propelled me across the rain-slicked street toward the churchyard steps.

"What are you doing?" My heart was in my throat.

"Going to take a look at it. Got to clean the damn blood off first."

"Here?"

"Got a better idea? Nobody's here."

"It's raining," I protested weakly.

He didn't respond. He didn't stop in the yard. The doors were off the chapel vestibule. Looters, I supposed; the nave was stripped bare. Even the pews and kneelers were gone.

Our wet, squeaking footsteps echoed raucously over the empty black-and-white checkered floor and across the high, vaulted ceiling.

He let go of me in the corner below an empty niche. Late morning light slanted in through arched windows high above us. The thrushes were still singing stubbornly in the yard.

"It was just the light," I told him. "It's fine."

"Like hell."

"You shouldn't say that here."

He dropped beside me. His blue, blue eyes lit on my hands and lingered for a second. "Where did you get that?"

I was still clutching his Saint Constantine. I had almost forgotten. I held it out to him hastily. "It's yours—I think. I'm sorry. It was in your room."

He took it on his palm as though weighing it. "My mother's," he said. "Stole it from her icon corner when I left home."

Guilt gnawed a hollow in my stomach. I was glad he was looking at the saint, not at me. I didn't think I could bear to look him in the face just now.

"Bet she's happy you've got him with you." My voice was hoarse.

He shoved the saint into a pocket. His jaw was tight.

"Yeah," he said. "I bet."

He reached for my head, positioning it just so in the light. He wiped blood carefully from my hairline with his coat sleeve and leaned close, scowling in concentration. His fingers brushed across my cheek. Gingerly, he felt along the side of my face—temple, brow. My breath caught. I squeezed my eyes shut.

He paused. I could feel him studying me. "Did that hurt?"

My teeth chattered. I clenched them fiercely. "No."

He pressed his fingertips along my cheekbone. "Here?"

"No. That, um—helps, actually." I drew an unsteady breath, touching my tongue to my dry lips. I turned my head back toward him. "Don't stop."

He went very still.

I opened my eyes. His fingers were still on my face—five little points of pressure on my cheek and ear and jaw. We were so close now that I could feel the halting shiver of his breath and see the widening black of his pupils.

I reached a tentative hand to his face, curling my fingers along his jaw, running my thumb gently over his cheekbone.

He swallowed. "You—you want me to—"

"Yes." My heart was in my throat again, pounding like a drum. "Please."

He hesitated. His fingers were trembling. He shifted his grip and made a cautious little move, dipping his head. Then he drew back again.

He looked away.

"I don't know if I—"

My heart stopped dead.

"It's all right," I said too quickly. "I only meant—if you wanted to. Only if you wanted to. It's all right."

"I want to," he said. "I want to."

I shook my head. My face was burning. I was sure he could feel it. I swallowed my heart back down, pulled away from his grip, and brushed my fingers quickly across my cheeks as if I could brush the shame away. "You're hurt. I'm sorry. Your knee."

"No, it's just—" He shut his eyes and opened them as if to clear his head. "I've never done it before."

"What?"

"Kissed anybody. Kissed a girl. I've never done it before."

It was such an earnest confession, and he looked at me so pleadingly, that I didn't dare laugh, but he must have known I was trying not to. I wanted to laugh—not at him, not really. I wanted to laugh for sheer relief.

"I've *been* kissed," he offered defensively. "Just—never *started* it."

"How'd that work?"

"On a mission. Part of the cover. It was a public place. She kissed me for cover."

"I'll bet she did." I'd bet that wasn't the only reason. She had probably been glad for the excuse, whoever she was. I felt a sudden, inexplicable twinge of envy. "So—never in school? Never kissed a crush?"

I could tell I had said the wrong thing. His gaze faltered.

"No," he said. "Left school when I was twelve. Mama needed me home."

Oh, I was an idiot. I had forgotten. "Because your father—you said the Reds—"

"Yeah."

"I'm sorry."

He shrugged a little. He was studying the floor tiles.

"My first kiss was Karol Nowak," I told him quietly. "The boy they shot in front of the constabulary office for not having a hunting permit."

"I know."

I stared. "You knew he was my first kiss?"

"I know who he was." His brow creased in a little scowl. There was an edge in his voice that hadn't been there before. "Lyudya did his dishes."

"What?"

"My sister Lyudya. She did six days a week for them. Three zlote a week."

I had been in the Nowaks' house plenty of times. I used to go over for French lessons with Karol's sister Adela; the Nowaks had a tutor come down from Dubno on Tuesday afternoons. I had never noticed a housemaid. I never had a reason to look.

I was too mortified to admit that to him.

"I didn't know," I said stupidly.

He seemed embarrassed all at once. He looked away.

"There was this girl—when I was thirteen," he said. "Zosia."

"Zosia Wójcik? The constable's daughter?"

"Yeah."

"You and every other boy in Bród."

"Yeah." His throat worked furiously. "Hadn't ever dared talk to her in school. Hadn't ever dared *look* at her. But Saint John's Eve, when they put the wreaths in the river. I was the one who got hers out of the water. That's how I was going to tell her. Took it back to her. She was with her friends, a bunch of her friends. She wasn't alone or anything. I gave her the wreath and asked her—in Polish, I'd practiced—I just asked her if she wanted to dance."

"And she told you no?" My heart suddenly ached for him— thirteen-year-old Kostya practicing his Polish so he could ask Zosia Wójcik to dance.

"No, she didn't tell me anything. Got one of her big brothers and his friends over. Told them I needed a lesson. Should have just shut up and taken it then. But I hadn't done anything. I told them I hadn't done anything. I wasn't going to do anything. Just wanted a dance."

"What did they do?"

"Nothing much. Could have been worse. The worst of it was she stood there and watched. Didn't tell them to stop. Just stood there and watched. Put her wreath back in the river afterward." He shrugged again carelessly, but I could feel the tightness in him. "What I got for being stupid."

"You weren't being stupid," I told him softly.

"That was stupid."

"Zosia Wójcik was stupid."

"Well, she wasn't the one crawling home with the shit beat out of her, so——"

He cut himself off.

"Sorry," he said.

"Would it help if I started?"

"What?"

"The kiss." My mouth was dry; it came out a little hoarsely. My stomach was fluttering. "Would it help if I started?"

He looked up.

"Yeah," he said shyly.

So I did.

I shifted onto my knees, took his face gently between my hands, turned his head up, and kissed him.

It was just me at first—he seemed to be letting me do it, the way Lew had let me do it, just sitting there and taking it—but all at once he slid impatient fingers across the back of my neck and pulled me in close, trapping my lips with his, testing my resistance with his tongue. I opened to him, and he swept in—lightly and uncertainly at first, then eagerly, pouring himself into each stroke.

Oh—I could feel that kiss all the way down to my toes.

He let my mouth go finally, though he didn't lift his hand from my neck, and I didn't take my hands from his cheekbones. We faced each other. We were both trembling and breathless.

"Sorry," he said. His mouth twitched. "How's your head?"

"Better. Definitely better. That was—" I licked my numb lips. "Unexpected. Been thinking about that for a while?"

"Yeah," he said.

"Really?"

"Yeah."

I was joking. He was serious. Guilt twisted my stomach. Oh God—I thought I knew where we stood with each other. Could I have given him to Kyrylo if I hadn't been so very sure he would do the same to me, if our places were switched?

I dropped my hands from his face and looked away. "So I stab you in the back, and you kiss me."

He bent his head and pressed his lips cautiously to my cheek. "I know where your brother is," he said into my ear.

I whipped my head back, caught off guard. "What?"

"I know where your brother is."

For a second, I just stared at him.

"Alive?" I managed finally. *Please, God.*

"Yeah," he said.

"Where?"

"NKVD headquarters. They're putting him on the eastbound train tomorrow morning. Podzamcze Station."

"Where is Podzamcze Station?"

"Couple of kilometers." His voice was muffled. He was still busy with his lips and tongue—working his way slowly down my jaw. "Other side of the High Castle."

"How on earth—"

"She's a UPA rat—the officer. She knew me. That's how we got out."

"And you trust her?"

"That's how we got out," he repeated, starting down the side of my neck.

"All right, but there's a difference between letting you go and letting Tomek go." It was hard to *think* with his mouth on my neck and his tongue doing what it was doing. I slipped my hands over his shoulders to hold myself steady. "You're UPA. It makes sense. Why would she help Tomek?"

He paused at my collarbone. "Yeah—makes perfect sense. She lets us go and then sets a trap for us."

"Why would she help him?"

"I don't know, all right? Maybe he's a good kisser." He was irritated now. "Don't go, then."

"I'm just saying let's be careful."

Oh—that was a stupid thing to say.

"You don't think I'm being careful? This whole damn time. You don't think I've had to be careful? You don't think I'm thinking about what happens to my mother and my sister if I'm not careful? Because I'm thinking about it, believe me." His fingers twitched on the back of my neck. "Even if I didn't want that kiss, do you really think I would say no to you? I do anything you say."

I was still holding on to his shoulders—holding tight. I let him go. I had been holding him so tightly my fingers ached.

"They're dead," I said.

"What?"

"Your mother. Your sister. They're dead. They've been dead. They've been dead for a month. The day Tomek found us. The NKVD shot everybody in Dalszy Bród that morning. The whole village—machine-gunned them. Burned the houses." I swallowed against the knot in my throat. "It's my fault. I killed those NKVD soldiers. They must have thought I was UPA. Julian said—Julian said they knew there were UPA in Dalszy Bród, and they must have—they must have thought—"

"Stop," he said, "stop."

"I'm sorry. I'm so sorry, Kostya. I should have told you. I know I should have told—"

"*Stop.*"

"I had to find Tomek." It came out in a whisper. "Don't you understand? I had to find Tomek."

His fingers twitched again. He yanked his hand from my neck. His face was choked with fury.

His voice was quiet.

"Yeah," he said, "I got it. You don't give a damn as long as you get what you want. You know they probably shot Lew."

I didn't say anything. I couldn't say anything. Yes, I knew. Julian would. He would have shot Kostya. He would shoot Lew. I knew and didn't care. I had to find Tomek.

Kostya shoved himself away from me.

"Eight thirty," he said. "They're bringing him by car. She said he'll be in NKVD uniform." He pulled himself up against the wall. "There—that's all you wanted from me, isn't it?"

And he was gone, limping slowly off down the nave, dragging his bad leg.

And I let him go.

I had no excuses. I had lied to him; I had used him. I had no right to stop him.

Couldn't have stopped him anyway. I didn't have the Walther anymore.

19
KOSTYA

HE TOLD HIMSELF HE WAS GOING TO PEŁCZYŃSKA Street, to NKVD headquarters, to turn himself in—right up until the moment his feet stopped in front of Marka Street, number twenty.

Didn't even know how he got there. He was just *there*.

"Tell them we sent you," Marek had told him back in Malechów. "They're good people. Poles, all right? But they're good people. They'll help you. They won't ask questions if you tell them we sent you."

And he was lost and aching, and his knee was hurting so badly, and he was soaking wet and shivering in the rain, and the lights in all the windows looked so bright and warm and welcoming, and before he could stop himself he was climbing the steps and ringing the bell—and then there was nothing left to do but stand there on the threshold, leaning on the jamb, awaiting his fate.

This was it. He was done. He couldn't walk any more if he tried.

Footsteps came toward him on the other side of the door. Kostya straightened as best he could.

"Marek and Agata sent me," he recited in Polish when the door opened.

The man in the doorway could have come from the comic papers or maybe from the Reds' propaganda as a caricature of capitalism—short and stout, wearing a neat pencil mustache and a three-piece suit, clutching a bowler hat in one hand. Kostya half expected him to lift a monocle to his eye.

"I beg your pardon?"

"Marek and Agata," Kostya repeated through gritted teeth. "They said to tell you—"

"Oh," the man said, "oh—I beg your pardon." He turned to call back into the house. "Renata! Here's another one for you." He opened the door a little wider. "Come in, come in."

"Mr. Jankowski was just leaving." Mrs. Kijek emerged from somewhere down the hall. "Hello again, Kostya. Do come in."

Kostya gaped.

"Come in, please, dear, before the rain does," Mrs. Kijek said briskly. "Stand on the carpet; take off your shoes. You'll leave tracks." She turned a blithe smile on Mr. Jankowski. "Goodbye, Zygmunt."

"Goodbye, goodbye." Mr. Jankowski gave her a neat little bow as he donned his hat. "Three days, then. Goodbye."

Kostya knelt numbly on the carpet to unlace his wet shoes. Mrs. Kijek waved Mr. Jankowski out and shut the door and bolted it.

"Last door on the right," she said to Kostya in Ukrainian. She swooped to pick up his shoes as she brushed past, heels clicking. "There are dry clothes in the wardrobe. Leave your wet things on the bathroom floor, please. I'll be in to take a look at that knee."

He hadn't gotten a word out yet. She must have seen the limp or something in the way he knelt. He hobbled awkwardly in his stocking feet down the long hall to the bedroom. It felt like a dream, all of it—real but *wrong*, like a morphine dream. The pieces were right, but they were all in the wrong place. He shut the bedroom door and closed his eyes and opened them. He half expected to be back out on the street in the rain when he opened them. But no—he was still there in the bedroom in his stocking feet.

He had never seen a bedroom like this, with tall glass windows and a four-poster bed the size of a hay wagon and a fat stuffed armchair big enough for four of him and a wardrobe the size of a whole other room—everything dark, glossy wood and clean white paint and soft, expensive fabric and electric lights. *He* was the piece in the wrong place; that was the problem. He felt small and dirty in that room. He felt like a snot-nosed little kid. He didn't even dare move from the doorway. He just stood there against the shut door, staring at that room.

He was still standing there when Mrs. Kijek knocked.

"I didn't know where the bathroom was," he explained stupidly. "You said to put everything in the bathroom."

She swept past him indifferently and opened the door in the wall beside the wardrobe.

"This is your bathroom," she said.

He went to look, bewildered. It was right there next to the room. It was almost as big as the room. There was a tub and a vanity and a toilet, all just right there.

His bathroom, she said. The only way you could get to it was through this bedroom. There weren't any other doors. *His* bathroom—which meant there were others.

"Never mind that now. It can wait," Mrs. Kijek said. She put her nurse's bag on the desk and pulled the desk chair out. "Sit— here. Not on the bed, not in those wet things. Roll your trouser leg up. Let me see."

He sat obediently, cuffing his trouser leg up over his knee. She held the knee between her hands, her face expressionless. She searched it over with cool, strong fingers and swung it thoughtfully back and forth. She reached for her bag, dug around for a second, and brought out a thermometer.

"Under your tongue," she said. "Lips shut."

"What does it say?" Kostya asked when she took it out. He wanted to show her he knew what it meant, the temperature.

He was proud of knowing. Lew had shown him the way the mercury rose and dropped and how to read the degree markings.

"Thirty-seven," she said.

"No fever?"

"No fever." She wiped the thermometer and put it back in its case. "No infection. You've had good treatment. Your knee hurts because the muscles have atrophied."

He was lost again. "What does that mean?"

"It means you haven't been using it and now the muscles need to be strengthened again."

"So all I have to do is use it?"

"To exercise it," she corrected. "Gradually, not all at once. You need to work back up to using it."

She took a bottle from her bag and measured syrup carefully into a spoon. Kostya stiffened.

"What's that?"

"Acetaminophen."

"To knock me out?"

"It won't knock you out. It's a pain reliever—a mild pain reliever."

"I don't want it."

"It will help the muscle pain."

Kostya's hands clenched. "I don't want it."

She gave him one quick look—one quick, hard, calculating look.

"Very well," she said.

She didn't ask questions. There was a stretch of awful, awful silence while she tipped the syrup back into the bottle. Kostya fidgeted.

"You knew I was coming," he said.

She returned the bottle to her bag. "No. But I've learned never to be surprised by who shows up on my doorstep."

"Oh. I thought maybe Marek told you I was coming."

She went into the bathroom to rinse the spoon. "Did he tell you to come?"

"He gave me the address. Didn't say it was you. Guess he didn't know I'd know you."

"I'm not usually here," she said, coming back into the room. "When the Germans were here, they requisitioned this place for officers' housing. I've been letting some of my daughter's friends use it since then. Marek was probably thinking of them." She tucked the spoon into the bag. She brought out another little bottle and showed it to him. "Iodine. You don't get to say no to this. Arm on the desk, please."

He hadn't even noticed the scrapes on his wrists where the handcuffs had bitten into him. He put his arm on the desk. She swabbed a piece of iodine-soaked gauze around his wrist, turning his arm over and back as she worked. She didn't say anything. She didn't look up. Kostya ached with the need to talk. Anything to break that silence. The silence was like fingers around his throat.

"Do you——" he started stupidly.

"Yes?"

"Nothing," he said.

She patted dry gauze over his wrist. "You can talk, Kostya."

He squeezed his eyes shut. It was like that stupid game where you pretended people couldn't see you if you couldn't see them.

"They're dead," he said. "Mama and Lesya are dead."

"I know," Mrs. Kijek said.

"You heard? About Dalszy Bród?"

"Yes."

He realized in that moment he'd been hoping Maria was lying. But there wasn't any benefit to her that he could see—lying about it. She'd gotten what she needed; that was it. No more reason for him to think Mama and Lesya were alive in Rivne. No real reason to tell him they were dead either, but definitely no reason to tell him they were dead unless they really were dead and it really had been the NKVD.

He guessed that was his consolation—that it was the NKVD, not Tomek. Not Tomek's squad. Not Lew. That he hadn't sat for three weeks in that bunker sharing cigarettes with one of the men who'd done it. That was his consolation. She wouldn't have said anything if it had been Tomek.

"Didn't even get there. Didn't even get to see them." He swallowed. "I should have been there. Should have been with them."

"*Should have* isn't for any of us to say," Mrs. Kijek said.

"I should have been with them."

"Other arm," Mrs. Kijek said.

He let her pull his other arm across the desk. His throat was tight. The anger had shriveled to ashes somewhere inside him. Now it was just the ache.

"Didn't know where to go," he said. "Didn't know what to do. Don't know what to do."

She finished swabbing his wrist and put the gauze in the wastepaper basket. She was still holding his arm in one hand. Just for a second, her fingers squeezed tight. Then she patted his arm and let him go.

"The first thing you're going to do is change out of those wet things," she said.

* * *

He couldn't stay, Mrs. Kijek said—not here in the city, not without identification. She had friends outside the city who would take him in until they could get photographs done and Mr. Jankowski could make new identity cards for him. (That was what Mr. Jankowski did, Kostya learned, and that was why he had been here, picking up somebody's photographs from Mrs. Kijek.) She couldn't take him up today because she had a meeting at the general hospital that afternoon. She would take him by car in the morning.

After that, they would have to see.

He knew what that really meant, "We'll see." That meant she didn't know what to do with him after that either.

She said he could go anywhere in the house and eat anything

he wanted in the kitchen cupboards while she was gone to her meeting, as long as he stayed away from the windows and kept the lights turned off, and she showed him how to turn on the gas for the hot water so he could draw a bath if he wanted. He couldn't go out. If anybody knocked on the door, he wasn't to answer. If anybody *came in* the door, he was to go out the back door into the courtyard and all the way across the courtyard to the monastery grounds, and from there to the coffeehouse on the boulevard, and she would come for him there as soon as she could.

That was just in case—just being safe. Didn't really matter, any of it. He didn't leave the bedroom, and nobody came.

She got back at half past nine. The bell at City Hall had just tolled. The clock out in the hallway was still tolling. It was running slow because it hadn't been wound in a while. He was just sitting there in the dark on the floor beside the desk. He had been sitting there all afternoon. He was wearing clean, dry clothes from the wardrobe now, but he didn't dare muss up that bed with the soft, expensive sheets. He listened to her moving around, switching on lights, opening doors. Her heels clicked up and down the hall, in and out of rooms. She came down the hall and knocked on his door. He didn't answer. The lights were off. She would think he was in the bed asleep. Part of him wished she would come in anyway. But she didn't. She went away back up the hall and switched the light off.

He didn't know why he hadn't answered.

He wished he'd answered. She would come in brisk and businesslike and ask whether he had eaten, and he would tell her yes just because, and she would know just by looking at him that he was lying, and she would make him eat anyway, and she wouldn't take his excuses about mussing the bed, and he wouldn't dare risk another one of those hard, calculating looks, so he would climb obediently into that bed and fall obediently asleep, and then it would be morning and they would be in her car going to her friends outside the city, and then he wouldn't have to think about any of it ever again—Maria or Tomek or Lew or the eight-thirty train at Podzamcze Station—because he would never see any of them ever again.

But he hadn't answered, so now he was just sitting here thinking about it.

He had been sitting here all afternoon thinking about it, and he would be sitting here all night—thinking about whether when he'd left Maria there in the church, angry and aching and still breathless from that kiss, he had known that was it, he was never going to see her again.

He didn't think he had known. If he had known, he wouldn't have left her. Wouldn't have told himself that stupid, stupid lie about going to Pełczyńska Street to turn himself in to the NKVD. He wasn't ever really going to Pełczyńska Street. He'd damn well known *that*. But he'd been angry—too angry to see things clearly. Too angry to remember he would have done the same thing, in her place, if it were Lyudya.

Too angry to realize he couldn't blame her.

He wished he hadn't left her.

He wished she had stopped him.

She hadn't. That was that. That was why he was sitting here thinking about it instead of going back.

He did fall asleep finally. He woke up once with a start, his head full of the sound of bombs, and he waited for the air-raid sirens and the drone of engines and the pounding of the anti-aircraft batteries, but all he could hear was the low gusting of the wind and the tapping of rain on the windowpanes. There were no more air raids, and it was just a thunderstorm. He went back to sleep, and when he woke up again it was morning. It was still dark in the room because the blinds were closed, but he could hear Mrs. Kijek in the kitchen, listening to the wireless while the teakettle warmed. The hall clock was chiming three quarters. Kostya sat there drifting slowly, slowly awake to the soft hiss and crackle of static and the tinny murmur of radio voices and the rush of steam in the kettle and the tapping of the rain. It had been raining all night.

Somebody pounded on the street door—pounded with a closed fist, *thud-thud-thud-thud-thud*, fast and loud like machine-gun fire—and he was awake all at once.

Mrs. Kijek switched off the wireless and moved the teakettle off the stovetop. Her heels went clicking unhurriedly up the hall. Kostya slid across the floor to put his ear against the door. The street door opened and closed. A jumble of noises came down the hall—low, urgent Polish voices, booted footsteps, ragged breaths. One long *thud* as if something heavy had been dragged in over the threshold. Somebody coughed wetly. The voices and footsteps got louder. They were coming down the hall. "Here," Mrs. Kijek said, "carefully—no, on the floor," and another voice, oddly familiar, said, "I've been doing everything I could, but—" and Mrs. Kijek said, "Are they looking for you, Tomek?"

Tomek.

Tomek's voice.

"Not yet," Tomek said, "hopefully not for a couple more hours, but I need the Fiat."

He was here.

He was here—three meters away on the other side of the door, here in Mrs. Kijek's house.

The hall clock had chimed three quarters—8:45—and Tomek was here. Not at NKVD headquarters. Not at Podzamcze Station. Not on the morning train. *Here.*

Which meant—

Maria.

Maria, wounded, gasping for breath, because he'd left her to go alone.

Kostya stumbled up, clawing the door open. He limped into the hall. They were in the bedroom across the hall. He came up short in the doorway.

Distantly, the bell at City Hall was tolling eight.

Eight o'clock. Not nine.

And it wasn't Maria lying there limp and shivering on the floor.

It was Kyrylo.

20
KOSTYA

MRS. KIJEK SAW HIM FIRST.

"My bag, Kostya," she said calmly. "In the kitchen."

He couldn't move. He stood there like an idiot. Mrs. Kijek was holding one of Kyrylo's arms across her lap, holding his hand gently while she peeled away strips of old bandage. Every one of Kyrylo's fingers was smashed to bloody pulp.

"My bag, please, Kostya," Mrs. Kijek said.

"I'll get it," Tomek said, putting Kyrylo's other arm down. He jumped up. "Come on, Kostya." He clapped a heavy hand on Kostya's shoulder and half pushed, half dragged Kostya out of the room.

He hauled Kostya into the kitchen and shoved him up against the wall, hard.

He pulled a pistol from somewhere inside his coat, snapped the action, and put the mouth of the pistol to Kostya's forehead.

"Three seconds. Where is she?"

"What the *hell*?"

"Two. Where's Maria?"

"Probably at the station. That's where *you're* supposed to be, so—"

"One."

"No—wait. Listen. Just listen." He couldn't get the words out. He couldn't think. "Nataliya—she said Volkov was sending you to Moscow. She said if we went to Podzamcze—she said she could make sure you were on the eight-thirty train at Podzamcze. She said you would be on the eight-thirty train."

"So why are you here?"

"How about why the hell are *you* here?"

"You knew not to go, didn't you?"

"What?"

Tomek's fingers knotted in his collar, pulling tight. The pistol pushed cold and hard between his eyes.

"Answer me. You knew not to go to the station."

"No—wait—that's not—" He didn't know what the hell he was supposed to know; that was the problem. "We had a fight. She said—Maria—she said you would let my mother and my sister go. She said if I helped her find you, you would let them go. And then yesterday she told me—she said—she said—"

The pressure on his throat eased just a little.

"She told you about Dalszy Bród," Tomek said softly.

"You lied to me." The anger came rushing back all at once. "You told her to lie to me. You knew they were dead."

"I knew."

"Better if I didn't know, right? Made me useful?"

"I wanted you to have the truth, Kostya. I wanted you to believe the truth."

"You should have told me, right? Yeah, that's exactly what Maria said."

"I didn't want you to hear it from an enemy," Tomek said.

"That's a load of shit."

Tomek's face was blank. "A month ago, would you have believed I didn't do it?"

"I'm supposed to believe you now?"

"You believe me, I'll believe you."

"What the hell does that mean?"

"It was a trap," Tomek said, "the station, the train. And I'm supposed to believe you didn't know. So I'd say we're just about even."

He lowered the pistol and let go of Kostya's collar.

Kostya swallowed. "That doesn't make any sense. Why the hell—"

"It isn't Nataliya's fault. She played into Volkov's hand. We all did." Tomek moved around the kitchen, opening and closing cabinets. "Volkov was never putting me on that train. But it was a good way to do some testing for leaks. All he's got to do is see who shows up at Podzamcze at eight thirty, and he'll know he's got a hole somewhere." He slammed another cabinet door shut. "Nataliya figured out what he was up to, but we didn't have any way to warn you."

"So how did you get out?"

"She forged release orders in Volkov's name." Another door slammed. "Where the hell is that bag?"

"They'll trace that back to her. She should have come with you."

"She said she didn't want Shukhevych and the UPA putting a price on her head. There's a price on Kyrylo's."

"Yeah, well, she said she wasn't going to let the Reds put a bullet in her head for you, so—"

Slam. "They won't."

"That's stupid. It'll take them two minutes to figure out who forged those papers. I bet they already have."

Tomek dragged the bag out of one of the cabinets and shoved it into Kostya's arms.

"Take this to Mrs. Kijek. Tell her I'm taking the Fiat to the station. I'll be back for you and Kyrylo. If I'm not—the Kostyshyn farm, outside Kulików. Mrs. Kijek knows it. They'll be able to help you."

"No."

"What?"

Kostya's throat was tight. "I'm coming with you. I shouldn't have left her—shouldn't have—"

"Do me a favor. Save it for her," Tomek said.

21
MARIA

THE BELL AT CITY HALL WAS TOLLING 8:15.

No sign of an NKVD staff car. No sign of Tomek.

No sign of the eight-thirty train yet either. It was supposed to be in at 7:35, coming in from Brody. The ghastly weather had thrown everything off schedule.

It was pouring. It had been pouring all night. There was a crowd jammed under the cover of the train shed. Military or medical personnel, all of them. They weren't letting civilians on any of the trains, except for a couple of men in suits who I assumed were local Communist Party officials. Most of the soldiers were regular infantry, but there were plenty of NKVD too. That was nothing unusual, I knew. They kept tight security at all the railway stations because of the risk of sabotage.

The Resistance and the UPA both targeted the rail lines pretty regularly, mostly doing what I was trying to do—disrupt the Soviets' prisoner transports.

I imagined that was why there was such a crowd here, at Podzamcze: The central station, on the other side of town, had been closed for months. This was the only functional station in Lwów.

They still made me nervous, the NKVD.

I didn't dare wait at the station. I was too conspicuous with my civilian clothes and my short hair and bruised face. I was sitting at the bar across the street, keeping an eye on the crowd. I asked the girl at the counter whether I could stand and wait for somebody, just to be out of the rain. I didn't have any money, and I imagined she could tell. She told me to sit and brought me a cup of tea anyway. She came back a little later with a piece of toast on a plate—no butter or jam, of course, but glorious hot toast just the same. I wondered whether she could hear my stomach growling. I hadn't eaten anything since the warehouse yesterday morning.

8:20. I could see the station clock from here.

No train. No car. No Tomek.

For the hundredth time this morning, I wondered whether Kostya had been lying.

For the hundredth time this morning, the sick twist of guilt in my stomach reminded me *he* wasn't the liar.

For the hundredth time this morning, I wished he were here.

Stupid, of course—stupid and selfish. I had made my choices. He had made his.

"Would you mind?"

I looked up. He was about Tomek's age, the boy standing there smiling at me. He was smartly dressed—suit and coat and hat and gloves, all good quality. He had a warm, handsome smile—the kind of smile that made you smile back and reach up to run fingers through your hair automatically, no helping it.

"I'm terribly sorry," he said. He spoke very proper Polish—crisp, enunciated. I couldn't place his accent, but it wasn't the local Galician. Somewhere northern. Varsovian, perhaps. He was moneyed and educated. A student? Had they even reopened the university?

"Would you mind?" he repeated.

Belatedly, I realized he was pointing with one gloved hand. There was a newspaper on the counter under my plate and cup—the Soviet paper, the *Red Banner*. I moved the dishes off hastily, brushing away the crumbs with the side of my hand, and slid the paper over to him. My cheeks were burning.

"I'm sorry—I'm sorry. Here."

"That's all right," he said. "It isn't even really news. Good for a laugh, though."

It was a bold thing to say. It was a stupid thing to say in a public place, especially with a station full of NKVD soldiers just across the street. I looked right into his face, caught off guard. He smiled again. Heaven, he had a beautiful smile.

"Augustyn," he said.

And a beautiful name.

"M-Maria," I managed hoarsely.

"Maria Kamińska," he said. "Yes, I thought so."

I spent a split second wondering where on earth he knew me from—and how on earth I could forget him—before I realized he had a pistol pulled on me.

"There's a car by the curb," he murmured. "We're going to walk out and get in the car. That's it, all right? No need to make a scene."

Nobody else noticed. Nobody was looking. The bar was practically empty at this hour even in the rain, and he was keeping the pistol carefully out of sight below the counter. The girl had vanished into the back. Was she the one who gave me up? Kept me occupied with tea and toast until she could raise the alarm?

No—that didn't make any sense. I had been sitting here for almost an hour, and there was a station full of NKVD soldiers just across the street.

Augustyn took my elbow and pulled me gently off the barstool, sliding behind me, pressing the mouth of the pistol into the small of my back. He kept his left arm looped lightly around my waist, holding me close against him. He was good: If anybody were watching, they would just think we were sharing a tender little moment. He bent his head to speak into my ear. His lips brushed my cheek.

"Walk," he said.

8:24. The train had just pulled in. I couldn't see it, but I could see the steam rolling up over the shed roof on the other side of the station building.

I hooked my foot behind Augustyn's ankle and threw my weight against him, backing him into the bar.

His feet flew up. He went crashing into the barstools. He let go of my waist by reflex, throwing out his left hand to catch himself on the counter.

I shoved away from him, staggered up, and ran.

He had recovered himself by the time I reached the door. He let off a quick shot as I stumbled out. The glass pane in the door shattered behind me. Somebody screamed. Across the street, a couple of soldiers were watching me curiously from the station platform—just smoking their cigarettes and watching, rifles slung. They weren't NKVD. They didn't seem inclined to brave the rain and interfere in this little squabble. Maybe they just didn't want to miss the train. They had been waiting for that train for almost an hour.

I whirled, trying to get my bearings. A car—he said there was a car.

There—on the corner, just out of view of the bar window, engine idling softly. It was unmarked black and the headlamps were off; it was hard to see in the downpour.

I took off down the sidewalk away from the car. Immediately, one of the car doors slammed. A Russian voice rang after me.

"Stoyat'!"

Halt!

I kept running. Augustyn's footsteps spilled onto the sidewalk behind me.

"Halt or we'll shoot!"

I kept running.

An engine roared. Another car—also unmarked, also black—pulled out of the side street just ahead, swung sharply toward me, and braked hard, squealing across the wet pavement.

I pulled up short. Oh God—shuttered shop fronts to my left, open street to my right. The soldiers on the platform had finally put out their cigarettes and unslung their rifles.

I was trapped.

Ahead of me, the car's passenger door flew open.

"Get in," Kostya snapped. He held the door open to shield himself. He had a submachine gun braced on the doorframe.

I lunged for the rear door and threw myself into the back seat, hauling the door shut behind me. Bullets sprayed across Kostya's door and up over the fender—*thunk, thunk, thunk*. Kostya let off one answering burst from the submachine gun and slid back in.

Tomek was at the wheel.

"Tomek," I gasped stupidly.

"Hello, Maja," he said over his shoulder.

"How on earth—"

Another spray of bullets rattled across the nose of the car. Tomek shoved the gearshift into reverse and floored the accelerator.

The car lurched backward. Something heavy slammed into us with another *thunk*.

"Was that the tires?" Kostya asked.

"Curb," Tomek said. "Sorry. Hang on."

"Do you want me to—"

Bullets spattered across the windshield. Kostya's head snapped back, then dropped. He slumped forward, forehead hitting the dashboard with a sick *smack*.

I reached for him without thinking, leaning over the seat.

"Get down," Tomek snapped.

"Tomek—"

"Damn it, Maria, get your head *down*."

I dropped numbly, digging my fingernails into the seat leather, looking at Kostya through the little gap between the seat and the door. He wasn't moving. *He wasn't moving*. He was slumped over his knees against the dashboard. His blood was all over the passenger window. Tomek spun the wheel under one hand, shifted, and floored the accelerator again. We shot into the side street, tires screeching, and sped away from the station.

Tomek reached over with his free hand to pull Kostya up.

"Shit," he said softly, "shit."

I had never heard him swear like that before. He held Kostya against the seat, his arm across Kostya's chest. "Hold him up," he said to me. "Keep his head up. Keep pressure on the wound."

I scrubbed at my face, brushing the tears away. "Where?"

"Under the collarbone. Right side. I don't think it's the artery, but you need to keep pressure on it. Here—take him. I've got to shift."

I slipped my arms around Kostya over the seat, pressing my palms to his collarbone. Blood dribbled out between my fingers. His coat and shirt were already soaked through. He felt limp and hollow and lifeless in my arms.

"What if it is the artery?"

"Just keep pressure on it."

"Tomek . . ."

He looked back at me in the mirror. It was the first time I had really gotten a look at his face. His skin was pale and thin, as if it had been stretched out tight over the bones. There were faint old purple welts in a line down the side of his face, disappearing down into his collar.

"We're going for help," he said. "We're going for help right now. He'll be all right, Maja."

I swallowed fiercely. I *would not* cry. "How did he find you?"

"Long story."

"I told him about Dalszy Bród. I had to tell him."

"I know."

"I lied to him. I told him they were in Równe—his mother, his sister. I told him they were at headquarters in Równe. I told him we would let them go if he helped me find you."

"I know," Tomek said.

"He told you?"

"He told me."

"I thought I was making it right," I whispered. "I thought I was making it right—telling him the truth, letting him go." The tears were coming out again anyway. I couldn't stop them. "I let him go, Tomek. He shouldn't have been here. He shouldn't even have been here."

"Save it for him," Tomek said.

22
MARIA

IT SEEMED TO TAKE FOREVER, THAT DRIVE, BUT
really it took about thirty minutes.

We had to do some weaving around to avoid the checkpoints
on the main roads. Once we were out of the city, it was a straight
shot. There was a safe house outside the village of Kulików,
just north of Lwów. It belonged to a Ukrainian family named
Kostyshyn. Friends of friends, Tomek said. Good people. The
oldest girl, Anna, was a Red Cross nurse. We could stay with
them until we figured out our next move.

They pulled Kostya away from me in the yard and bundled
him into the kitchen. I tried to go with them, but Anna pushed
me out and shut the kitchen door in my face.

"Wait," she ordered.

So here I was in the Kostyshyns' sitting room, clutching a cup of linden tea, waiting.

Waiting and waiting and waiting. The tea had been cold for half an hour.

Tomek was gone. He had gone with one of the Kostyshyn boys to hide the car and cover the tire tracks on the road from Kulików. I had no idea where he got that car. He told me most of the story while we drove—how he had shared a cell with Kyrylo Romaniuk, how the UPA girl Nataliya had forged release papers for both of them when she realized the train plan wasn't going to work, how he had dragged Kyrylo five blocks from NKVD headquarters to the house of a Resistance friend and had found Kostya there—but there were still some bits and pieces missing. They weren't important so I hadn't asked.

Another boy was here with me in the sitting room. He wasn't a Kostyshyn. The whole crop of them—I had counted five so far—seemed to have the same dark brown hair and laughing eyes and round, dimpled faces. This boy looked like Tomek—dust-colored hair cut close to his scalp, high-boned serious face. I thought he *was* Tomek at first glance. At second glance, he was too small and too tanned and a few years too young. He was perhaps a year or two older than I was. But he had the exact same serious look, the exact same little philosophical furrow to his brow. He was sitting very quietly across the room from me—just sitting, looking out the window at the rain. There was a heavy plaster cast on his right foot.

"Is it broken?" I asked him finally in Ukrainian. I needed to talk. This sitting and waiting and not knowing and not being able to *do anything* was unbearable. All I could hear from the kitchen was the occasional metallic clinking of instruments on a tray, and all I could think about was Kostya's blood spattered on the car window and the *smack* of his forehead hitting the dashboard.

The boy looked at me. Oh—and he had Tomek's way of making you think he could cut you into pieces with one glance. Not hostile, just assessing. Reading and filing carefully away. He looked startled that I was talking to him more than anything. He blinked.

"What?"

"Is your foot broken?"

"Shrapnel," he said. "It's almost better now."

A wound, not a break. He didn't really seem to mind that I had asked, but I wished I hadn't.

"Oh," I said stupidly.

"I can speak Polish if you want."

I didn't know whether to be offended. "Is my Ukrainian really that bad?"

"It's pretty good," he said with the solemnity of a professor giving marks.

"But you knew from about three words that I'm Polish."

"You told them your name was Mar-ya. In Ukrainian it's Ma-ree-ya." He darted another glance over me. "My mother was Polish. That was her name. She said it like that—Mar-ya."

"What's your name?"

"Tolya," he said.

"For Anatoliy."

"Yeah."

"Do you live here with them? The Kostyshyns?"

"Just for a while. Just until I can take the cast off. Anna says I can take it off in a couple days."

We both looked at the cast critically.

"What was it?" I asked, curious despite myself. "You mean shrapnel like a shell fragment?" I asked in Polish because I didn't have the vocabulary in Ukrainian to talk weapons.

"Grenade," he said, also in Polish.

"Does it hurt?"

"Not anymore. Itches sometimes. It was a couple weeks ago."

He was deliberately avoiding details. He didn't want to talk about it anymore—or he couldn't for security reasons, I supposed, not knowing me. Maybe he just didn't have the vocabulary in Polish.

I wondered whether he was UPA.

"We have a cousin named Anatoliy," I told him. "Or we had. Except we said Anatol. That's the Polish."

He was looking out the window at the rain again. "Dead?" he asked quietly.

"I don't know," I admitted. "Mama tried keeping up for a while before the war, but her letters kept coming back. And then Papa said she shouldn't write."

"Why?"

"Well—they were on the other side of the border. On the Soviet side. Papa didn't like her writing."

He absorbed this expressionlessly. "Where?"

"What?"

"Where on the Soviet side?"

"Kuz'myn—outside Płoskirów. That's where Mama was from, actually. That's where her family was from."

"I was born in Kuz'myn," he said.

He looked at me. We studied each other.

"Your mother—"

"Maria Sikora," he said.

"She was my aunt—my mother's sister. I'm named for her." My breath was caught in my throat. "Anatol. You're *our* Anatol."

He was so still, so silent, his face so carefully blank, that I was afraid I must have hurt him somehow.

"I'm sorry. Anatoliy. I didn't mean—"

"Anatol," he said.

"What?"

"You can say Anatol. She always said Anatol—my mother." He swallowed. "You can say Anatol."

I let out my breath in a nervous, shivery little laugh. "You look so much like Tomek. I thought you were Tomek. No wonder."

"Who is that?"

"Tomek—my brother, Tomek. Tomasz. You probably saw him. He was driving the car."

"Oh," he said.

Then he said, "Is it just you?"

"You mean—"

"Just you and him?"

"Oh—yes. Now. Mama and Papa are dead." I swallowed. "And you said—Aunt Maria—you said *was*—"

"Yeah," he said.

"And your father?" I didn't even know his name.

"Yeah."

"I'm sorry."

"It's all right," he said. "It was when I was a kid." As if that made it all right somehow.

"I wish we had known." I did—suddenly and fiercely. "I wish we could have done something."

"It's all right," he said.

I hated the way he said it so automatically—*it's all right*. I hated to think he actually believed it. None of this was all right.

"Did you even know about us?"

"Mama never talked about her people much." He hesitated, giving me a cautious glance. "My grandmama wrote sometimes. Guess she was your grandmama too."

"Grandmama Elżbieta. In Lwów."

"Yeah."

"We tried to write. Mama did. The letters just kept coming back. And Papa—"

I cut myself short. I didn't want to tell him what exactly Papa said about Ukrainians and Reds and about Mama's sister for choosing to live with a Ukrainian, and a non-Catholic one at that.

"Yeah," Anatol said.

He wasn't looking at me. I had the feeling he knew anyway.

Boots clomped on the front stoop. Tomek came in from the yard with the Kostyshyn boy, Ivan. They were both dripping wet and muddy, carrying their boots in their hands.

"Road's flooded all the way back to Kulików," Tomek said to me shortly. He wasn't happy. His brow was furrowed in that little scowl.

"Isn't that good?" It meant the NKVD couldn't track us.

He and Ivan put their boots carefully on the pieces of old newspaper spread over the floor by the door and came into the room in their stocking feet. Ivan vanished down the hall to get towels from the washroom. Tomek dropped heavily onto the floor beside my chair. He wiped rain from his face with the backs of his hands and leaned his head back against the wall. He was exhausted.

"Kyrylo's still in Lwów," he said.

"You said he would be all right with your friend."

"Well, I thought she was going to be able to get him here." He kneaded his temples with his fingertips, eyes shut. "Thought of everything but the damn roads. Can't get him any farther than Kulików until the road dries out."

"They can bring him by the river," Anatol said.

He had been sitting there so quietly since Tomek came in that

I don't think Tomek had even noticed him yet. I think he thought we were alone. His eyes snapped open.

"That's how they brought me," Anatol said.

"Tomek, this is Anatol." My throat was tight. "He's—"

"Aunt Maria's kid," Tomek said.

I faltered. "You knew?"

Tomek didn't answer right away. He bent to peel off his wet socks. His shoulders were stiff.

"I asked her why she did it," he said finally. "Nataliya. I asked her why she forged those release papers for us. They were her death warrant, and she knew it. I couldn't figure it out. I asked her why." He tossed his socks onto the newspaper one after the other. "'Ask your cousin'—that's all she said. 'Ask your cousin when you get to Kulików.' She had my file. She'd seen Mama's name—Sikora."

He looked up at Anatol.

"It wasn't for me—what she did. It wasn't for us. It was for you."

Anatol sat very still. He was looking at his hands. His face was blank.

"Is she dead?" he asked.

"She's dead," Tomek said.

Anatol looked at his hands very intently. "They couldn't kill her," he said. "She wouldn't let them kill her."

"She didn't," Tomek said.

"How?"

"She'd wired explosives in the offices. She knew the NKVD would trace the release orders back to her. She knew the UPA would put an order out for her once they found out she'd blown her cover to help me escape. This was checkmate."

"You saw it?"

"I saw it. I saw what was left. There weren't any survivors— not in the offices. The upper stories were blasted clean." Tomek's voice was quiet. "I'm sorry, Anatol. I wish this didn't have to be the way we met. I wish this didn't have to be the reason."

Anatol brushed his hands on his trousers and looked out the window.

"It's all right," he said. "There were just some things I wanted to tell her."

23

KOSTYA

HE THOUGHT HE WAS BACK IN THE BEDROOM AT
Mrs. Kijek's house at first, coming awake slowly to the tapping of
rain on the window and the soft, crackling sputter of a wireless.
He lay there for a stupidly long time, bleary-headed, blinking up
at low wooden rafters, before he realized he wasn't.

Those rafters were wrong. The close plank walls were wrong,
and the bare single-paned window was wrong, and the darkness
outside the window was wrong, and this bunk—this low, narrow
bunk with its threadbare old quilt and stiff straw mattress—was
very wrong.

He didn't know where he was. Couldn't remember how he
got here. That was bad.

He wasn't alone. That was worse.

Somebody else was with him in this dark little room, listening to the wireless on the wall shelf. The low, flickering light of an oil lamp threw eerie, distorted shadows all over the walls.

He tried to move. That was a mistake. Sharp, sharp pain jumped across his chest and burrowed deep under his collarbone. He dropped back against the mattress, gulping a little.

"Easy," somebody said.

That voice. He remembered that voice.

He remembered waking up to that voice—waking up just like this, dazed and aching and helpless, blood in his mouth and panic in his throat.

Ask me to stop it and I'll stop it. All you have to do is ask.

Kyrylo was sitting on the end of the bunk, smoking a cigarette. The tip flared softly red as he inhaled.

Kostya thrashed reflexively. *Mistake, mistake, mistake.* Pain burst through him with a vengeance. He curled up against it, pulling his knees in, making himself small. He lay there shivering and wheezing in the quilt. It was a dream. It had to be a dream. Kyrylo wasn't here. Kyrylo was a pile of bloody pulp on the floor of Mrs. Kijek's spare bedroom, and this wasn't Mrs. Kijek's house.

So where was it?

It's a dream. It's a dream. It's a dream.

It felt real, all of it. The pain felt real.

The tube in his arm felt real.

He followed the tube with numb, slippery fingers. There was

a catheter stuck in his forearm just below his elbow. There was a drip pole standing by the bunk. He fumbled at the catheter, heart thudding, stupid with the panic.

Somebody's hand slid over his arm in the dark.

Kyrylo's hand. The fingers were splinted.

"Hey. Don't do that," Kyrylo said.

"Take it out."

"Nothing doing."

"Get it out of me."

"Do you even know what it is?"

"Get it the hell out of me."

"Just shut up and lie still. It's three in the morning. Nobody wants to listen to you."

Door hinges creaked. A dark-haired girl poked her head into the room. She was in a nightgown. Her hair swung in two long, dark braids over her shoulders.

"What's wrong?"

"Nothing," Kyrylo said. "Everything's fine. Sorry we woke you up, Anna. Go back to bed."

She came in anyway. She went over to switch the wireless off. "Have you been up all night?"

"No," Kyrylo said.

"You're an awful liar." She took his cigarette, stubbed it out, and handed the stub back to him. "Go on—get some sleep. I'll sit with him for a while."

Kostya watched warily while she came over to the bunk. She

sat on the edge of the bunk and pulled Kostya's arm across her lap. She held his wrist in her hand, pressing with her thumb to count the pulse. She was about Kyrylo's age. She had a kind, tired face. She gave Kostya a kind, tired smile.

"How are you feeling?"

"Take it out."

"I'm sorry?"

"The drug. Whatever it is. Take it out."

"The plasma?"

"Whatever the hell it is."

"It's not a drug. Plasma is the liquid in your blood. We're giving you a transfusion until your body can make up the blood loss."

That stumped him.

"Blood loss."

"You were shot—here, just under the collarbone. It missed the subclavian artery, so it's not as bad as it could have been. But it's bad enough." Her voice was quiet. "Do you remember?"

"No."

"Well, you got a pretty nasty bump on your head too."

"Who are you?"

"Anna. Anna Kostyshyn. I'm a nurse."

The name seemed familiar—Kostyshyn—but he didn't know why. Everything seemed blank and blurry outside the four close walls of this room. "Where am I?"

She put his arm down and laid a cool hand on his forehead.

"You're safe. You're in my house—my family's house. This is my family's farm."

"How?"

"What?"

"How did I get here?"

"They brought you here—do you remember? Maria and Tomek brought you here."

Maria. Tomek.

The station. The rain. Wet brakes squealing. Gunfire.

"Is she here?"

"Maria? She was in here earlier."

"Can I see her?"

"She's sleeping now. It's late. You ought to be sleeping too. I can give you something if you want."

"No."

She sighed. "No—Kyrylo said you probably wouldn't."

"Are you with him?"

"I'm sorry?"

"Kyrylo. Are you with him?"

She tilted her head a little. "I'm not sure what you mean."

"You've got to go. You've got to tell them to go."

Her brows drew down into a questioning little scowl. "What?"

"You and Maria and Tomek. You have to tell them to go before Kyrylo knows."

"Before Kyrylo knows what?"

"Before he knows you helped me."

"I think you need some sleep," she said.

"Listen to me. You've got to go. He'll kill you if he knows you helped me."

"No, he won't."

"Listen to me. Please."

"I extracted that plasma from Kyrylo's blood, Kostya. He asked me to." She draped a quilt over him and went to turn the lamp down. "Nobody's going to kill anybody for helping you. Try to sleep."

* * *

He didn't sleep. He hurt too much to sleep. But he closed his eyes and pretended, lying very still and breathing very slowly and deeply, because he was afraid Anna would give him something if she saw him lying there awake.

She was awake the whole time, sitting on the big chest in the corner, knitting something. Kostya couldn't see her, but he could hear the rhythmic *click* of the needles. Every now and then she would get up and go out, moving quickly but being careful not to make any noise with her footsteps. She would come back a few minutes later and sit back down with her knitting. After a while she would get up and go out again. He could hear her being sick outside the door. He wanted to sit up and tell her it was all right, she could keep the pot in the room; she didn't have to keep going out. But he didn't want her to know he was lying there listening to her.

Kyrylo came back in a little before dawn. The room was still dark except for the dim glow of the oil lamp, but a rooster was crowing somewhere.

"Please tell me you slept," Anna said softly.

"Little bit. Sorry to make you give up yours."

"I was up anyway."

"Takes after its father, doesn't it? Keeping you up nights."

"You're unbelievable."

"How's the kid? Mine, I mean."

"Out—the way you should be."

"I'll bet he is." Kyrylo's voice was dry.

"You need to tell him, Kyrylo."

"You want me to wake him up?"

"No. I want you to stay and tell him."

"Not my decision. Kamiński wants to get as far downriver as we can before—"

"He can stop pushing himself so hard too. Both of you could use the rest. *All* of you."

"Take it up with Kamiński."

"I will." Anna slid off the chest, bare feet thumping on the plank floor. "And you can stay here and talk to Kostya."

Her footsteps went away across the floorboards. The door closed behind her. Kyrylo came over to the bunk. He stood over the bunk for a moment, fumbling with a cigarette. Kostya lay very still under the quilt, eyes squeezed shut. The trick was the way you breathed—long and slow in, long and slow out . . .

Kyrylo yanked the quilt off of him.

"Can't pull that one on me, idiot. I know you're awake."

"Go to hell," Kostya said.

Kyrylo sat down on the edge of the bunk. He was holding the cigarette awkwardly between thumb and index finger because of the splints. The lamplight carved deep, dark hollows into his face.

"Already been," he said.

Kostya looked at the wall. "Why did you do it?"

"Do what?"

"She said it was from you. This stuff." Kostya flapped his arm against the mattress. The drip pole jerked a little.

"She needed somebody who matched your blood type. I was the winner. Don't get all mushy."

"Why did you do it?"

"Were you listening?"

"You know damn well that's not what I mean."

"You'd better watch your tongue. She's a lady—Kamińska. You want a chance with her, you'd better stop talking like a boor."

"Answer the damn question. You know I ratted you out to Marko."

Kyrylo took a long drag, eyes narrowed. "Yes—I figured that one out."

"You said you'd kill me if I ever ratted you out."

"Let me ask you a question." Kyrylo knocked the ash carefully from his cigarette with one splinted finger. "Did you ever think about how Marko knew who you were? You never told him your name. Did you ever think about it?"

"He was there. He was there when I came asking you for help finding Lyudya."

"You came asking *us* for help," Kyrylo corrected. "That's what you told him. You were looking for your sister at the transit camp, and you wanted our help. He had no idea who you were. He knew you were a security problem. You'd come to us. You knew things. You'd seen faces. You'd heard names. That meant either you stayed, or we shut you up. But you didn't give a damn about the UPA. All you cared about was finding Lyudya. You told Marko to his face, remember?"

Kostya didn't say anything. He did remember. That was back when he thought he actually had a choice.

"He put it together—why I wouldn't kill you. Why I wouldn't let him kill you. Why I made you stay and join up when the easiest thing would have been a bullet in your head. He was an idiot, but he put it together. He knew I was trying to protect you. Didn't take him long to figure out why." Kyrylo pulled on his cigarette. "Did you ever think about why he wanted you on his circuit? He could keep me in line as long as he had you. And I was afraid—if you ever figured out what he was doing—I was afraid you would do something stupid. This is you we're talking about. I was always afraid you were going to figure it out and do something stupid— try to kill him, try to kill yourself, trying to *help*. So . . ."

He shrugged.

"Two and a half years of doing absolutely everything I could to make sure you hated my guts. Sooner or later I was going to push you too far. It wasn't your fault, Kostya."

Kostya looked back at the wall. "You mean sooner or later you knew I was going to rat you out."

"I wouldn't put it that way. I didn't *know* anything. I planned for contingencies."

"Solovey was there on your orders, wasn't he? You ordered him to be there—to get me out."

The tip of Kyrylo's cigarette flared red.

"I planned for contingencies," he repeated.

"So he knew." Kostya swallowed. "He knew it was all a lie. Everything I told him—everything you said about Mama and Lesya—everything you told me you were going to do if I crossed you—"

"He knew."

"Why didn't he tell me?"

"You wanted out, idiot. We were getting you out."

Kostya looked at the wall.

"Didn't do any good," he said. "Didn't do any good anyway."

"Did some good. Got you out of the way so I could take care of Marko."

"Mama and Lesya are dead," Kostya said to the wall.

Kyrylo pulled on his cigarette.

"So—something I need to tell you," he said. "That message— the one from Nataliya. Remember that?"

"What?"

"The message from Nataliya in the bar. The thing that started all of this. Know what it was?"

"What the hell does that have to do with anything?"

"It was a copy of an NKVD order. Straight from Moscow. Instructions for dealing with *us*. 'UPA combatants to be publicly hanged if captured. Associates of suspected combatants to be deported to labor camps.' Family, that means—'associates of suspected combatants.'" Kyrylo flicked the ash from his cigarette. "Nataliya had to slip it to you in person because command decided it was better we didn't know—better for morale. They were worried about mass desertions if word got out."

"So?"

"So. I cleared out the cache after I killed Marko. She'd left us a list of names—deportees from Volyn, from L'viv. This was from the end of July, maybe the thirtieth or the thirty-first."

Kostya curled his fingers into fists, digging his fingernails into his palms. Every part of him was wound up like tension wire, stretched too tight, ready to snap. "And?"

"Their names were on the list. Klara and Lesya Lasko." Kyrylo's voice was quiet. "They weren't even there that morning, Kostya. They weren't even in Dalszy Bród."

"Alive"—in a whisper, heart lumped in his throat. Hoping and not daring to hope.

"Alive."

He snapped all at once. He choked out a laugh. Maybe it was a sob; he didn't know. "The labor camps."

"We'll get them out."

"How?"

"I don't know. But we will. Kamiński's got contacts. Kijek's got contacts. High-ups in London and Washington. We'll get them out." Kyrylo hesitated. "There's a trade-off, obviously."

"I'll do anything. I don't care."

"Don't be stupid. What do you think I meant—we were going to swap you for them? Kijek thinks she can get you British citizenship. She thinks that will help with the negotiations—if we can say you're a British citizen." Kyrylo pulled on his cigarette absently. "The thing is—she thinks she can get you the citizenship as a political refugee. I imagine that means they've got to *believe* you're a political refugee. Which means—"

"Going to England."

"Not necessarily England." Kyrylo let out a long, smoky breath. "But you won't be going home for a while."

THE HOUSE WAS ODDLY QUIET.

It was midmorning. It felt earlier than it was because it was still dark out—a cold, damp, gray morning, heavy with the threat of more rain. Tomek and Kyrylo had left in the boat at daybreak. A couple of the Kostyshyn boys went with them—Ivan and another identically dark-haired, dimpled boy whose name I was hopeless to remember—so they could bring the boat back. Anna said she wasn't a surgeon by specialization and Kyrylo's fingers needed somebody who was if he ever wanted to use them again for anything besides holding a cigarette.

They were taking him to Lew.

Tomek shut himself in the attic with Anna's Red Cross radio transceiver all yesterday afternoon. The dratted rain must have been playing havoc with the signal. He didn't emerge until suppertime. I didn't know what exactly he had said to them or what they had said to him. Lew was alive. That was all that mattered. Tomek was going to make a recommendation to command that he be cleared of any charges. There wasn't any question that he *would* be. Just a formality, Tomek said, for Lew's sake. Lew believed very strongly in formalities.

I should have gone with them. I should have been apologizing to Lew myself. That was the least I could do. I owed him so much. We all owed him so much. At the very least, I should have apologized to his face. I liked to think it was because there literally wasn't any more room in that little boat, not because I was a coward.

There would be another time. I had to believe there would be another time. I had to believe sooner or later this war would be over and there would be time for all the things I didn't know how to say.

Anyway, Tomek said if he knew Lew at all—and he did—Lew would tell me there wasn't anything to apologize for.

And he would tell me he knew why I stayed.

Anna was coming out of Kostya's room on tiptoes, shutting the door very softly behind her. They had been trying to get Kostya to sleep all night. He wouldn't take the pain medications, and he was apparently very good at pretending to be asleep. The only way you could tell, Kyrylo said, was that when he was really asleep his mouth was usually open.

"Is he—"

"Yes—finally." Anna gave me a weary little smile. She said she was up nights anyway because of the baby, but I was pretty sure part of it—the part she wouldn't admit to—was just that she didn't trust the job to anybody else. She let Kyrylo sit with Kostya a bit last night, I supposed because Kyrylo was family. But she was back in there as soon as Kyrylo was gone. "I was just going to slip out and get some tea."

"I can sit with him for a while," I offered innocently.

She drew up on full alert.

"I'm not going to wake him up," I promised.

She hesitated.

"Please," I added stupidly.

Her face softened just a little.

"If you wake him up, I'll kill you," she said.

She didn't have to worry: I couldn't have woken him up if I tried. You couldn't have woken *me* up last night if you had been shooting at me with howitzers, and I didn't think he had gotten much more sleep these past few days than I had—except for that little bit under Marek's cart bed, and I didn't imagine that had been very restful.

I wanted to wake him up—don't get me wrong. I wanted to wake him up and tell him I was sorry, so sorry, and then I wanted to shake him by the shoulders and ask him why—why on earth did he come back, and how on earth could he be so very *stupid*, and didn't he understand I was letting him go?

I didn't, of course. I had the feeling he wouldn't answer me anyway—just give me that stupid little shrug and scowl at the wall until I dropped the whole thing.

There would be another time.

I did the best I could for now, which is to say I leaned over him carefully and kissed him very gently on the cheek. I supposed that was really everything I wanted to say anyway.

LIST OF MILITARY AND PARAMILITARY FORCES

Gestapo—Geheime Staatspolizei, the Nazi secret police

NKVD—Narodnyĭ Komissariat Vnutrennikh Del (People's Commissariat for Internal Affairs), the Soviet secret police from 1934 to 1946, eventually succeeded by the KGB

Polish Resistance—collective name for the armed forces of the Polish underground state that fought German and Soviet occupation in Poland

Silent Unseen—Cichociemni, an elite group of Polish special-operations agents trained in Britain and parachuted into occupied Poland to help lead Resistance efforts there

SS—Schutzstaffel (Protection Squadrons), originally Hitler's bodyguard, expanded into an elite Nazi security force responsible for implementing racial policies

UPA—Ukrainska Povstanska Armiia (Ukrainian Insurgent Army), the military arm of the Ukrainian nationalist movement, fighting at various times against the Soviets, the Germans, and the Polish Resistance alike

LIST OF CHARACTERS

MARIA "MAJA" KAMIŃSKA, returning home to Bród, Poland, after two and a half years as an *Ostarbeiter* in Rüsselsheim, Germany

KOSTYANTYN "KOSTYA" LASKO, returning home to Bród, Poland, after two and a half years as a courier for L'viv Group of the UPA

UPA

ROMAN SHUKHEVYCH, commander

MARKO, commander of L'viv Group

KYRYLO ROMANIUK, nom de guerre Lys, Kostya's cousin, squad leader

DIMA BARANETS, Kyrylo's second-in-command, and Dima's wife, YULIYA

SOLOVEY, squad leader

ANDRIY, Solovey's second-in-command

NATALIYA, UPA mole embedded in the First Ukrainian Front of the Red Army

POLISH RESISTANCE

TOMASZ "TOMEK" KAMIŃSKI, nom de guerre Robak, Maria's brother, Silent Unseen and leader of Wydra Squad

EDEK, JULIAN, LEW, and TADEUSZ, members of Wydra Squad

MAREK and AGATA, farmers

RENATA KIJEK, Resistance member in Lwów

ZYGMUNT JANKOWSKI, Resistance member in Lwów

OTHERS

FYODOR VOLKOV, comrade colonel of the NKVD's 64th Rifle Division

Kostya's mother, KLARA LASKO, and his sisters, LESYA and LYUDYA

INNA, resident of the apartment building where Kyrylo Romaniuk keeps a safe house

AUGUSTYN, NKVD agent in Lwów

ANNA KOSTYSHYN, Red Cross nurse, and her family

ANATOL, guest of the Kostyshyns

AUTHOR'S NOTE

The seeds of this story were planted when I read Vasily Grossman for the first time in an undergraduate history class in 2012. The passage from *A Writer at War* that appears as this book's epigraph has haunted me ever since. It raised questions that I had at that point never seen answered in fiction about World War II: After "liberation," what happened to the millions of Eastern Europeans—many of them children, some as young as ten—who were taken by the Germans for use as a massive slave labor force in German factories and on German farms? How many of them managed to make it back home to Russia, to Belarus, to Poland, to Ukraine, and reunite with their families? How many of them managed to make it back home only to find that home and family were no longer there?

The process of researching my previous book, *Traitor*, and learning more about these slave workers (the Germans called them *Ostarbeiter*, Eastern workers) made me determined to write something about them, and I owe a great deal to Sophie Hodoro-wicz Knab's book *Wearing the Letter P* for providing insight into what my Maria's experience might have been like. At the same time, I was reading Stephen Rapawy's *The Culmination of Conflict*, which describes some of the instances toward the end of World War II in which units of the Polish Resistance and the Ukrainian Insurgent Army (UPA) put aside their mutual hostility and cooperated in joint operations against Soviet forces.

One key figure in peace talks between the Poles and the Ukrainians was Marian Gołębiewski, a Polish army soldier who escaped occupied Poland and made his way circuitously to England via Romania and France. He was one of the Cichociemni, the Silent Unseen, trained in Britain by the Special Operations Executive and then parachuted back into Poland, where he commanded units of the Polish Resistance in the Volhynia region. He and his willingness to work with the Ukrainians—sometimes against the wishes of the Polish government-in-exile and his superiors within the Resistance command structure—became a source of inspiration for my Tomek.

Eventually, all of these disparate elements—*Ostarbeiter*, the Silent Unseen, cooperation between the Polish Resistance and the UPA—came together in this story. Some of the details are fictional: The villages of Bród and Góra are made up, though based on real villages destroyed by the UPA between 1943 and 1945, in particular Hurby and Huta Pieniacka. The main characters are all fictional, though inspired by real people and experiences. But the heart of this story—reconciliation between former bitter enemies—is, incredibly, a historical truth.

Many thanks to Isaiah McCrina, Elizabeth McCrina, Kaye Acosta, Mary Johnson, Marte Mittet, Gabriella Saab, Olesya Gilmore, Marina Scott, Rose de Guzman, and Eva Seyler for reading and giving invaluable feedback on early drafts; to my agent, Jennie Kendrick, for all of her encouragement and support; and most of all to my editor, Wes Adams, for letting me write yet another story with a bunch of acronyms and difficult Slavic names.